King of the Trenches

Ghost & Tranay Adams

Lock Down Publications and Ca$h
Presents
King of the Trenches
A Novel by *Ghost & Tranay Adams*

Ghost & Tranay Adams

Lock Down Publications
Po Box 944
Stockbridge, Ga 30281

Visit our website @
www.lockdownpublications.com

Copyright 2021 by Ghost & Tranay Adams
King of the Trenches

Lock Down Publications
Like our page on Facebook: Lock Down Publications @
www.facebook.com/lockdownpublications.ldp
Book interior design by: **Shawn Walker**
Edited by: **Shamika Smith**

3486288288Thank you.

Stay Connected with Us!

Text **LOCKDOWN** to 22828 to stay up-to-date with new releases, sneak peaks, contests and more...
Thank you.

Submission Guideline.

Submit the first three chapters of your completed manuscript to ldpsubmissions@gmail.com, subject line: Your book's title. The manuscript must be in a .doc file and sent as an attachment. Document should be in Times New Roman, double spaced and in size 12 font. Also, provide your synopsis and full contact information. If sending multiple submissions, they must each be in a separate email.

Have a story but no way to send it electronically? You can still submit to LDP/Ca$h Presents. Send in the first three chapters, written or typed, of your completed manuscript to:

**LDP: Submissions Dept
Po Box 944
Stockbridge, Ga 30281**

DO NOT send original manuscript. Must be a duplicate.

Provide your synopsis and a cover letter containing your full contact information.

Thanks for considering LDP and Ca$h Presents.

Let Me Holla At Chu!

   This piece was by far the hardest I had to write in my entire career. I find that interesting since I was splitting the duties with Ghost, whose pen I respect! I had so much going on within my life that I found it difficult to complete my portion of it. It seemed as if I'd never get done with it, but thankfully, that time finally arrived.

   This will be book number fifty for me, which would make me halfway to my goal of completing 100 books before I die. I'm actually happy about that. Hell, I'm smiling while typing this. I'd like to thank you all that have supported me during my time in this industry. Every last one of you has pushed me to finish a new book or series with your reviews, compliments, and words of encouragement. I cannot thank you all enough. I hope I did not forget anyone. If I did, I'll get you on the next one. Forgive me, Pimps fuck up too!

Acknowledgements

Judith Sims, Michelle Harvey, Jane Pennella, Dorothea Creamer, Tia Fanning, Tanya Garry, Jeannette Frazier, Helene Young, Lulee Kitty, LeShe Beckham, Eliza Tellis, Juanita Taylor, T.J. Edwards, Jelissa Edwards, and Joan Brooks.

My Self-Published Works

The Devil Wears Timbs 1-7
Me and my Hittas 1-6
The Last Real Nigga Alive 1-3
A South Central Love Affair
A Hood Nigga's Blues

Chapter 1

It was a sweltering night in New York as heavy rain descended from the heavens, adding to the muggy atmosphere. Lightning flashed across the sky every three seconds, followed by a thunderous boom that resonated across the entire borough of Manhattan. Jabari, a caramel-skinned, one hundred seventy-five-pound man with a low haircut and a temper more lethal than a man on steroids, pulled the all-brown stolen Chevy Astro van into a huge alley located behind the expensive mansion. He cut the engine, took the all-black ski mask from his lap, and slipped it over his head after drinking the remainder of the mixed Lean inside of his Sprite bottle. His eyes were low and menacing. He flexed his muscles and rolled his head around on his neck. "Yo, my nigga, you ready to make this shit happen?"

Paperchase ran his tongue across his front teeth, the four gold fangs shined brightly in the dimly lit van. He slid his mask over his dark-skinned face, shaking his head from side to side, allowing his long dreads to flow freely down his back. He stood six feet tall, born and bred in Brooklyn, and addicted to the drill scene. Those that knew him well referred to him as a stepper. He was quick to slide up to any opp and empty his clip. He'd jumped off the porch early. The murder game had been instilled in him by his older brother, Scorpion, a Brooklyn legend. "Asking me if I'm ready is like asking a hungry lion if he's ready to feast on a vulnerable antelope that he already got his claws into. I live for this shit, my nigga. Let's move."

Jabari opened the van's driver's side door and stepped out of it. The rain was coming down so hard, his black hoodie matted to his waves in a matter of seconds. He grabbed his .45 from under the seat and tucked it into his waistband.

Paperchase jumped out of the van and stepped his left foot all the way forward, which allowed him to slide the big pump down his thigh. He kept the handle above his waist to make it easier for him to retrieve if he needed to. Together, the pair hunched down and made their way through the dark, rat-infested alley. Ignoring

the rodents, they proceeded on their way until they were at the back of the mansion, overlooking the patio doors that opened to the twenty-five-meter pool out back.

Jabari looked at the time on his cheap, waterproof watch and nodded. "Hopefully, shorty's ass doing what the fuck she's supposed to be doing. Either way, we are in this bitch in like five minutes."

Paperchase pulled the bottom part of his mask up and popped two Xanax. He closed his eyes and opened them clenching his jaw. He could already taste the blood that was sure to be shed. The rain popped off his hoodie, making his dreads nap up. "Scorpion said this bitch ain't new to the game. He taught her everything she knows, so we ain't gotta worry about her doing her thing. We just gotta do ours."

***

Olivia stepped in front of the full-length mirror and turned in a slow circle. She smiled at the way her red satin Prada panties cuffed her mound, exposing the meaty portion of her lips. She had on the matching bra that was see-through. Her large areolas were on full display just as she needed them to be. At thirty years old, the Puerto-Rican native had a figure that kept most men in Brooklyn salivating. Her strong accent was all thanks to her parents and San Juan, her birthplace. Olivia looked over her shoulders at Bret as he slipped his arms around her perfect body. "Damn, Papi. You almost ready for me, or are you going to sit around all day and shoot that shit up your arm?"

Bret Chambers was an ex-NFL football quarterback that was well renowned. He'd been at the peak of his career when suddenly it was ended by a scandal that had rocked his very brand. He could still remember the headlines. *Star Quarterback Sexual Romp Photos Released on Instagram.* All for the world to see. The pictures were more than damning and cost him four million dollars in legal fees and over two hundred million in civil court. Since the beginning of his legal battles, Bret had found himself surviving by the heroin he pushed into his system on a daily basis. He was up to

two grams a day and climbing. He'd lost all his family, most of his friends, and every endorsement deal that he'd ever landed. It was as if his career never happened. He was lucky he'd paid off his mansion when he'd had the funds to do so and kept a nest egg tucked away for when he really hit rock bottom, which he was sure was inevitable.

Bret licked his thin lips. The six-foot five-inch quarterback made Olivia look like a little girl as he held her within his arms. "I'm ready, babe. You already know how long I last when I have that Heaven pumped inside of me. I remember you crawling the walls pretty good." He sucked on her neck and humped into her backside.

Olivia pushed back into him and moaned. "Okay, Papi, well, I'm ready to tap out." She smiled devilishly.

Bret pulled his dick out of his boxer hole and ran it up and down her backside. His fingers slipped into her panties from the front, cuffing her juicy pussy. Olivia spaced her feet and leaned her head all the way back while he licked up and down the vein on her neck. "Stop teasing me, Papi. I want you now."

"Bitch, that ain't happening," Jabari interjected as he threw the wire around Bret's neck and tightened it with all of his strength. He started to move backward.

"Ahhhh!" Olivia screamed and dropped to the floor.

Bret threw his arms in the air at first, but then he tried as best he could to fit his thick fingers under the wire to gain some sort of relief. Jabari was having none of it. He pulled it tighter, jumped up, and locked his legs around Bret's waist. Bret's eyes bulged. He spit a thick glob of saliva. Olivia scooted backward on her ass. Bret carried Jabari across the huge living room and then ran backward as fast as he could, crashing into his China cabinet. Jabari fell off him with the wind knocked out of him.

"Fuck!" he gasped.

Bret threw the wire to the ground, inhaling a deep breath of air. His face was bright red, and the veins in his forehead were prominent. He looked down at Jabari with murder in his eyes.

"You motherfucker! Who sent you, huh? Was it the seventeen-year-old's parents? Was it my bookie?"

Jabari stood up, trying to collect himself. He reached for his gun only to find it absent. His eyes bucked. "Aw, shit." He threw up his guards. "Come on, you big muthafucka. Come on."

Bret lowered his head and balled his massive fists. He stomped toward Jabari. "I'm going to kill you and scream self-defense. This was your biggest mistake, motherfucker. Ahhhh!" He charged at Jabari, picked him up, and crashed him back into the China cabinet. Jabari hollered in pain. Bret grabbed him by the neck and balled up his fist.

Paperchase slid behind him and pressed his pistol to Bret's earlobe. "Bitch, that's royalty you're attacking. Not on my watch! Gang, gang!"

Boom! Boom!

Bret's noodles splattered all over the side of the cabinet. He staggered on his legs before falling sideways. A large puddle of blood formed around his head. Paperchase stepped over him, knelt down, and held his finger to his throat. There was a slight pulse. He took his trusted scalpel and slammed it into Bret's throat, slicing upward before downward again. Bret kicked his legs straight out, seizing before dying. Paperchase helped Jabari to his feet.

Jabari dusted himself off with a mug on his face. "Damn nigga. What the fuck took you so long?"

Paperchase wiped his scalpel off on Bret's cheek. "I wanted to see how you were going to handle yourself. I told you to slice his throat and fuck the wire. That shit takes too long."

Olivia stood up and kissed Paperchase on the cheek. She dug into her blouse and handed him the codes to all of Bret's safes. "Here you go, Papi. I don't know what's left. That muthafucka owes everybody."

Paperchase nodded and took the paper from her. "Y'all go upstairs to grab that shit. I'ma clean up down here. Hurry the fuck up, though."

14

They followed his orders to a tee. When it was all said and done, they left fifty thousand dollars richer, not counting the two hundred thousand dollars in jewelry that was confiscated by the trio. Though thirty thousand would go to Scorpion and the majority of the Woo crew out in Brooklyn that were in need of canteen, lawyer fees, and help for bill money for their families that were still on the streets, Paperchase knew that it was a necessity that the job had been pulled. It was the way of life, and since he was next up to be crowned king, he had to formulate and execute each mission with extreme precision.

Ghost & Tranay Adams

16

Chapter 2

It was a bright and sunny day outside of the Red Hook housing projects. A five-foot seven-inch, browned-skinned, short dread-lock sporting, fifteen-year-old named Ramone stepped outside of the buildings. He stopped mid-step as his eyes closed in on Fat Juan and his hot dog cart that had all the buildings on lock.

His specialty was a turkey Frank wrapped in bacon with nacho cheese sauce, jalapeños, onions, and mayonnaise. Ramone's stomach growled like a vicious mountain lion. He was tired of him and his older brother, Jayshawn, being forced to eat meals that were basically scraps. Things like syrup, mayo, and ketchup sandwiches, ramen noodles, and cold hot dogs because the gas and lights had been turned off months ago.

He nodded as he watched Fat Juan wrap a hot dog in bacon and serve it to a thin Spanish woman with a plump rump. "Yo, I don't give a fuck what the bidness is today. Word to the Gods, I gotta have me one of those joints. Fuck the dumb shit." He pulled up his shorts and tightened the electric extension cord around his waist that he used for a belt. Kneeling down and tying his shoes, he tried his best to ignore the fact that his right toe was close to poking through the hole there. After both laces were tied, he casually strolled up to the hotdog vendor. Fat Juan took his handkerchief and wiped his face with it. He stopped to wring out the sweat from it before setting his eyes on Ramone.

Ramone sized him up quickly. "Say, Fat Juan, let me get one of your specials, Pa. Word to God, I'm hungrier than a fat bitch right now."

Fat Juan tucked his handkerchief and squirted hand sanitizer into the palm of his hand. He slid on a pair of latex gloves and started to put together Ramone's order. "It's scorching outside already. I don't know if I'll be able to maintain this heat, Lord knows." He shook his head and then took a moment to breathe.

Ramone glanced around the neighborhood. Though it was only nine in the morning, most of the dope boys were out along with the hot girls. The hustlers were posted up six and seven deep

with their car doors open, banging music. The hot girls strolled up and down the block, nodding their heads to the music. Some were pushing strollers, and others were in threes with their like-minded gold-digging buddies appraising each hustler. Jack boys looked down on the busy scene from the top levels of the project building, plotting and scheming. Little kids were chasing each other up and down the block while the dope addicts set out on their missions to generate revenue to feed a demon that was incapable of being full. This was Brooklyn!

Ramone's stomach growled at the scent of the bacon being wrapped around his hot dog. He watched Fat Juan spread the cheese and strategically place the jalapeños on it. It took all the willpower he had inside of him to not push the fat man over to run away with his cart.

While Ramone was imagining him doing so, Fat Juan finished his order. "What kind of potato chips and drink would you like?"

This is where Ramone's entire plan would come to fruition. He knew that nearly everybody around the borough hated Fat Juan's pineapple soda pops. It was the least requested beverage, and because it was, they were often placed all the way at the bottom of the cooler. "Let me get some sour cream and onion potato chips with a pineapple soda."

Fat Juan smiled. "It's about time somebody ordered one of those. I'd hate to see them go to waste." He handed Ramone his food along with the potato chips. He opened the cooler and braced himself for the cold ice. He stuck his head inside of it.

Ramone wrapped his paper around his hot dog and took a step back before he ran full speed at Fat Juan, crashing into him and knocking the man into his cart. Ramone took off running. He didn't look back over his shoulder until he was half a block down the street. He was expecting to see Fat Juan just getting to his feet, but he got the shock of his life when he discovered that the street vendor was only a few strides behind him. He cursed and sped up, holding his hot dog tighter. He could feel the heat permeating through the wrapped hotdog.

"I'm gon' get you, nigger. Every day it's one of y'all screwing me over!" the Mexican man hollered, trying to pace himself.

Ramone ran across the street, still looking over his shoulder. He pushed a group of little girls out of the way that was jumping double Dutch. "Watch out y'all. Please, move!" he demanded.

Fat Juan reached and took hold of the back of his shirt. "Come here."

Ramone twisted and broke away again, but not before his entire shirt was half ripped off his body. He kept running. He hopped over a stray dog and slid across the hood of a tenant's car. He jumped off it and landed back in the street, looking back trying to locate Fat Juan. Before he could lay eyes on him, a teenage girl driving a purple Dodge Neon slammed on her brakes. Ramone turned to face her just in time. He hopped into the air, and the car rammed him hard, causing him to do a complete three-sixty in the air before he landed hard twenty feet from where he stood at first. Potato chips went all over the street.

"Fuck!" he hollered out, still clutching his hot dog.

Fat Juan stopped at the curb, struggling to catch his breath. He slowly made his way to the vulnerable Ramone. It was time for payback, and he didn't care who was watching. This dish of revenge promised to be served cold.

Toya came to Ramone's side with her hands planted to her face. "Oh my God! Oh my God! I didn't see him. He just ran into the middle of the street. I swear."

Fat Juan pushed her out of the way. "Move, his ass is mine. First, give me this, you thief." He snatched the hotdog out of Ramone's hand and tossed it aside. He balled up his fist and punched Ramone as hard as he could in the face.

"Noooo!" Toya screamed.

Fat Juan punched him three times hard. Then he slammed him to the pavement and slapped him across the face. "You dumb, nigger!"

Toya hopped on his back. Fat Juan stood up and shook her off him. He slapped her across the face and turned his sights back to

Ramone. He raised his chubby foot, ready to crush Ramone's ribs. "Let this be a lesson to all of you!"

Jayshawn came from the side of the street vendor and punched him so hard, he tripped over his own feet and fell to one knee. The sound of the punch resonated up and down Red Hook. Fat Juan dropped to the curb and hit his head, splitting it open. He crawled to his feet fast and upped a .38 Special, aiming it at Jayshawn.

Jayshawn threw his hands in the air. "Come on now, Juan. That's my lil' brother."

Fat Juan felt the blood slide down the side of his face as it dripped off his chin. He frowned and fired. "You son of a bitch!"

Boom!

The bullet slammed into Jayshawn's shoulder, knocking him backward. The onlookers took off, running in every direction. Fat Juan stepped over Jayshawn and fired again, popping him in the stomach. He was ready to pop him a third time when Jabari aimed from the doorway of the building and popped him twice in the midsection with his Draco. Fat Juan shook before he fell on his face. Jabari ducked back inside of the project building, but not before both he and Ramone had locked eyes. He cursed under his breath and hustled up the stairs. When he got inside of his apartment, he broke the Draco down into the smallest of pieces, stuffed them into a book bag, and was back out of the apartment. He fled the projects, heading for the Harlem River where the pieces of the Draco were set to take a dive.

Paperchase pulled up and hopped out of his red SRT. He was being followed by a van full of shooters. He ordered them to load both Ramone and Jayshawn into it. Once they were loaded and lying on the top of the plastic, the van sped away with them. Paperchase was familiar with the sight of Toya whenever he cruised through South Brooklyn. He helped her come to her feet. "Yo Goddess, what the fuck happened on my streets?"

Toya was crying so hard that it was difficult for her to catch her breath. "That boy came running into the middle of the street because that fat man was chasing him. I clipped him with my car, and that fat man beat him and me up. The fat man shot both of

them and then somebody had shot him. This is crazy. Brooklyn is getting out of hand." She sniffed blood back into her nose.

Paperchase nodded. "Yo, don't tell the Jakes none of that shit. We don't fuck wit' Twelve around dis joint. We live off street justice. Lemme handle dis shit, aiight?" He tilted her chin up so she could look into his brown eyes.

She agreed, "Aiight, Dunn. I'm about to get out of here. Can I drive away, or should I stay on the scene?"

Paperchase raised his right eyebrow. "Fuck you think?"

She backed away. "Okay, well, I'm out of here."

Paperchase waited until she pulled off before he stepped over the fat street vendor that was wheezing for air. The fat man turned onto his back and started to get up, holding his stomach where he'd been shot, thankful that the bullets had hit his bulletproof vest before they zipped into him. Blood oozed through his hotlink-sized fingers.

Paperchase looked around at the deserted streets. "You caused all of this commotion in my fuckin' borough?"

The street vendor came to his feet, hunched over. He stood in a puddle of his own blood. Fat Juan frowned as he heard the sirens of the police car. He knew that he was safe. "Fuck you, Maurice! Fuck you and all these apes around here. Why if I was ten years younger, I'd kick your Black ass." He spit a bloody loogie onto Paperchase's chest.

Paperchase looked down at it just as the police rounded the corner. He mugged Fat Juan. The police jumped out of the car and rushed over to them. Paperchase raised both of his hands, and with the left one, he gave a signal to one of his trusted young shooters in whom he was sure was watching the entire scene.

Fat Juan ran to the policeman clutching his stomach. "Help me. I was robbed and shot. That piece of shit over th–"

Bocka! Bocka! Bocka!

Fat Juan's face exploded all over the white policeman. The officer screamed like a chick in a scary movie before he took cover, looking up at the buildings. Paperchase disappeared into the

Red Hook houses with a sly smile on his face. Nobody fucked off in Red Hook without his say-so, nobody he told himself.

Chapter 3

Errrn! The loud buzzer sounded as one metal door after the next opened for Montell "Scorpion" Williams to make his way through the prison until he entered the hot and humid visiting room. He stepped inside and adjusted his prison-issued blues making sure he was tip top. The visiting room was packed with children and baby mothers galore. He searched through the sea of people until his eyes landed on Olivia and Paperchase. He smiled but then quickly erased the expression, remembering that Terre Haute was a maximum-security federal prison located in the state of Indiana that fed off weakness. So much as a smile was enough to get a man placed on the menu. It didn't matter if he was the king of the Woo or not. He stopped at the officer's desk, handed them his visitor's pass, and signed up to take pictures. After he finished, he navigated to where his people were seated.

Paperchase stood up first. He placed his fist over his mouth. "Look at my nigga. On gang, yo' bitch ass buff as hell."

"Fuck you thought I was gon' be, bitch. I gotta keep shit in order. They might've given me fifty years, but I got some shit in the works. I ain't finna be in this mafucka forever. That's on Woo 'nem grave," Scorpion promised. He hugged his little brother tighter.

Olivia stood up in an all-white Fendi dress so sheer that her areolas were clearly visible. The dress was so tight that it looked painted on. She smelled like Fendi as well. Her succulent lips were painted cherry red, looking glossed up and popping. "Daddy, you missed me?"

Scorpion stood at five-foot-ten with brown skin, long dread-locks, and full of solid muscle. "Hell yeah, boo, get yo' ass over here right the fuck now."

She almost tripped, trying to get over to him. She wrapped her arms around his neck. "I missed you so much, Papi. When are you going to get out? The streets ain't been the same without you?"

Scorpion kissed her lips. "I got some shit up my sleeve. I'll be home in no time. You just keep handling Daddy's bidness. You hear me?" He gripped her ass and pulled her further into him.

"Yo, I'ma go hit up the machine. Fuck you wanna eat, Boss?" Paperchase asked, trying to ignore Olivia squeezing and stroking his brother's dick through his prison blues.

"The usual, my nigga. On gang, get me a couple of pizzas, too. No swine, though," Scorpion ordered.

"Got you, king." Paperchase disappeared through the visiting room.

Olivia and Scorpion sat down with him sitting directly across from her. From this angle, he'd be able to see right up her dress all the way to her freshly Brazilian waxed pussy lips. It was the perfect visual for him. He picked up the bag of Flamin' Hots and felt around inside of the bag until he located his thirty balloons. He strategically placed them in his mouth, swallowing them back-to-back. Olivia looked out until he was finished. She opened the bottled water for him and smiled when he crushed the remaining chips inside and tossed them into the garbage.

Paperchase came back and laid the food all over the small table. He took a seat beside Scorpion, handing his brother a gang of napkins. "I made sure I packed the best heroin in New York. That shit got the fiends screaming for more. One percent fentanyl, too, mixed perfectly, though."

Scorpion nodded and looked between Olivia's thighs as she flashed him her juicy pussy. She spaced her knees further until he confirmed he could see her pink with a nod. He shivered. The two had been boyfriend and girlfriend ever since they were fourteen years old when Scorpion and Paperchase had moved over from Harlem. Olivia had been the finest girl at their high school, and Scorpion just had to have her. After knocking out and stomping her previous boyfriend, demanding that she be his, she had been. The two had been inseparable until three summers prior when Scorpion and twenty of his Woo Clique had been indicted for racketeering, money laundering, conspiracy, and weapons charges. Even then, Olivia had held him down every step of the way.

Paperchase looked over at Olivia and caught sight of her pussy as well. He cursed himself for getting an instant erection. He started to imagine all kinds of funerals, dead bodies, bugs, and even pulling a drill on some niggaz in order to take his mind off of the fact that her pussy was on full display.

Scorpion leaned forward. "Look, you two, I got another move lined up, and I need this shit taken care of right away. This one has a lot to do with my case, and it's Woo bidness. You muthafuckas gotta handle it strategically as a muthafucka, though. Any false moves and the Choo will get a firmer grasp of the streets, and the Woo will lose a lot."

The Choo were the Woo's sworn enemies. The war had started out from drill songs disrespecting each other's sets and dead homies before it blossomed into an all-out war for blood and supremacy. Now, it was murder on sight for both crews. The struggle was located in the heart of Brooklyn, and it grew by the hour.

"Yo, tell the God what the fuck you need me to do, and that shit is done. That's on the guys, nigga." Paperchase looked into his eyes.

Scorpion nodded. "That's why I love yo' ass, boy. We gon' get to it. But first, let me ask you a question. Keep that shit one hunnit. Olivia been one hunnit to me?"

"What?" When Scorpion posed the question, Olivia snapped out of her zone and sat up.

Paperchase looked across at Olivia and laughed. "Far as I know."

"Far as you know, huh?" Scorpion asked. "This is the only person outside of you that I have ever loved, Dunn. This girl still gives me butterflies every time I see her, even from across the room. On our mother, I'm not lying."

Olivia smiled. "What you think you be doing to me, Papi? I want you so bad. I thought you were going to pull some strings to get us married so we can have conjugal visits? What the fuck?"

"She's still hollering marriage. What a Dame, huh, Paperchase?" Scorpion laughed.

"That's your one, big bruh. That's all I can say." Paperchase took the top off of his Pepsi and drank from it.

"The warden signed off on it. I get the paperwork back sometime next week, and then we'll go to the next phase. You're gonna be my wife, shorty. That's gonna be the fuckin' day. Word up. Damn, I love yo' ass." Scorpion hated feeling so soft.

"I love you, too, Papi. Always have, always will." She cocked her thighs wider and blew him a kiss.

Scorpion stared at her for a long time before his facial expression became sinister. "Hand to God, if I ever find out a nigga fuckin' my bitch, I'ma kill you, Olivia, and that nigga's whole family. Bitch, you belong to me. It's always been us, and it's always going to be us. That's what it is, and it's final." He mugged Paperchase. "Nobody touches Olivia. Put the word out all over New York. You got that?"

Paperchase nodded, noticing the frown on Olivia's face as she crossed her thighs. "Indeed, I do."

Scorpion mugged her and started to grin viciously. "Okay, now you two listen up. This is what's next on the agenda..."

***

When Paperchase and Olivia arrived back at the hotel room that night, they were still eleven hours away from the time their plane was set to take off for New York. Paperchase opened the door for Olivia and allowed her to walk into the room. She stepped past him as he closed and locked the door. When he turned back to see where she was, she pushed him into the door and kissed his lips hard, her breathing rugged. Paperchase pushed her off of him. "Wait a minute, Olivia. I don't know if I can do this shit anymore."

She stepped back and looked him over. "What?"

Paperchase wiped her red lipstick from his mouth. "Yo, that nigga still bananas over yo' ass. I can't fuck him over like this. That's my brother, shorty."

Olivia stood for a moment staring at him. She started to shake her head slowly. "Nah, nigga. You don't get to do that."

"What the fuck are you talking about?" he snapped.

"You don't get to pick and choose when we are together and when we aren't. Nigga, you knew what it was the first time you got me to crawl into your bed. I told you right then that I wasn't the average female. I told you what it would be once you laid that thick dick on me. That's why I was hesitant for us to fuck around with each other because I already knew what would take place. Now, you got me here, and you think you about to kick me to the fuckin' curb because you're feeling a way. Nah nigga, yo' punk-ass belongs to me now. We're in this shit together." She stepped back into his face and ran her hands over his body. "Don't you want me just as much as I want you, Papi? I know the sight of him seeing my pussy turned yo' ass on. Nigga, you're just as crazy about me as he is.'" She dropped down to her knees and rubbed the front of his Balmain jeans.

Chapter 4

Olivia kissed the front of his pants and rubbed the side of her face against the material. "Talk to me, Papi. I need to know what you're thinking." She unzipped him and fished his dick out. It stood up like a sword pulsating, full of heat. She stroked him.

Paperchase was fighting between his carnal desires for her and the love that he had for his brother. It sucked that Olivia had been his first piece of pussy. Ever since she'd laid in his bed, she'd done some of the most disgusting and hypersexual things to his body that he couldn't explain. Turning away from her now was nearly impossible. He didn't possess enough willpower to do so. When she slipped him into her mouth, he wanted to slap himself from the moans that escaped his lips.

Olivia smiled with his thick shaft moving in and out of her mouth. She closed her eyes and slurped him like a savage. She had to keep him locked down. She was certain that it was all over for Scorpion, and Paperchase was the key to her continuing to live the lifestyle to which she had been accustomed. Scorpion had provided her with a champagne lifestyle, one she refused to depart from, especially after growing up with heroin-addicted parents who barely gave two shits about her. No, she couldn't see it. She sucked him faster and harder. Before he could bust, she stood up and stroked his dick within her little hand. She rubbed the head up against her dress. "You wanna fuck me, Papi, huh?"

Paperchase was fiending. He slammed her up against the wall and yanked up her dress. She yelped. Her pussy juices were leaking all down her thighs. He could smell her scent. The visiting room had been very humid, and she hadn't been given the chance to wash just yet, so she was a bit sweaty down there. The aroma of her drove him nuts. He dropped down and stuffed his face into her pussy, opening her lips wide.

"Unnnnn! Uhhhhh! Bro, please! Fuck. I'm supposed to be your sis. Fuck, baby." She rested her right foot on his shoulder and busted her cat wide open for his tasting. Paperchase went haywire. He tongue fucked her, sucking on her clitoris and rolling it all

around her pearl. He slurped up her juices and swallowed them as they came out of her. When she screamed and stuffed his face into her pussy even harder, he tensed and picked her up against the wall eating away. Olivia beat on his back, begging him to stop. Her clit was too sensitive. She needed a moment.

Paperchase slammed her to the bed and ripped her dress down the middle. He got between her thighs and ran his fat dick head all around her opening. Her lips puckered. He cocked back and slipped deeply into her forbidden walls, sighing in ecstasy. "'Damn, sis." He bit into his bottom lip as he fucked her as hard as he could.

Olivia closed her eyes tight and kept the back of her knees upon his shoulders. She could feel him digging deeper and deeper inside of her womb. She leaked and screamed. She grabbed the pillow and bit into it. "Unnnnn, Maurice! Maurice! Fuck me, lil' bro. Damn this pussy yours! It's yours! Ooooooooo, fuck, I'm coming!" she screamed as an orgasm coursed through her.

Paperchase slammed faster and harder. He eyed the insertion point. He watched his dick go in and out of her. Every time he pulled back, his piece appeared whiter and was full of her cream. He imagined the anger his brother would feel, and this caused him to roar like a mighty beast before he started to cum in thick jets back-to-back. "Aww, shit! Shit, sis!" He pulled his dick out and busted all over her again and again, splashing her neck, chest, and stomach.

Olivia laid down with her thighs wide open, rubbing the semen into her skin. "Fuck, I love you. Don't nobody do me like you do, Maurice. Fuck, we got a problem." She laid back and closed her eyes.

Paperchase got between her thighs and trapped her clitoris with his mouth, sucking until she locked her thighs around his neck. He nipped it while fingering her asshole, causing her to cum again, and screamed as she released him. Then they rolled around in the bed, kissing and hugging. It ended with Olivia lying on top of him, sucking on his ear lobe while she told him how much she truly loved him.

King of the Trenches

Ramone stirred in his sleep. Behind his eyelids, he replayed the incident with the street vendor all over again. He was halfway across the street when he felt a presence to the left of him—Toya's Dodge Neon. Before the car could collide with him, he hopped up and sat upright in the hospital bed with sweat pouring down his face.

Toya jumped up, dropping her knock-off Gucci bag to the ground. She rushed to his side. "Ramone, are you alright?"

Ramone squinted his eyes. The entire room felt to him as if it were spinning out of control. The morphine that pumped through his system had him high as gas prices and numb as a Republican.

Martha moved Toya out of the way. "Baby, are you okay?" The dark-skinned, skinny, five-foot woman asked her son. She reached to rub his back. All up and down her arm were full of track marks from her heavy heroin addiction.

Ramone trailed his eyes up to her and slowly eased her hand from his shoulder. "Yo, I'm good. Where is Jayshawn? How is he doing?"

Martha dropped her head. "He's still in the intensive care unit. Lord knows that I pray my baby pulls through. You two are my whole life," she cried.

Ramone wanted to disagree with that statement, but instead, he decided that he would let her have it. Though deep within his heart of hearts, he felt that Martha didn't care about anything outside of her heroin. For as long as Ramone could remember, it had been that way ever since Father Chico, their mother's ex-pimp, had turned her out on the drug before the two of them were even born. Ramone pulled his head back when she started to rub his face. He took her hand and guided it back to her. He had an IV placed inside of it. He looked past her and to Toya.

Toya locked eyes with him. Martha took a gander backwards and got the hint. She removed herself from the middle of their union. Toya stepped closer to the bed. "Hey, I'm sorry. I didn't mean to hit you. I was driving and making sure that I had the

entire street within my line of vision when you came out of nowhere. I sincerely apologize. Please forgive me."

Ramone shook his head. "Yo, if that clown wasn't chasing me, you would have never run into me. It's not your fault; it's his. I appreciate you coming down, though. That means everything to the God."

She smiled and placed a tuft of her curly hair behind her ear. She was light caramel with brown eyes and the femininity of a beautiful African barbie doll. "I mean, I had to be here. I didn't know what was to become of you. I've been so worried, plus I think we go to the same school. Aren't you a freshman at Frederick Douglass? "

He nodded. "Yeah, I just got there this year."

"Yeah, I'm a senior. I thought I recognized you." She sat on the edge of his bed. "Why was that man chasing you? "

Ramone shrugged his shoulders. "I don't know. I think he was a pedophile or some shit." He was too embarrassed to admit the fact that he'd been starving. "Yo, have you heard anything regarding my brother? "

Toya nodded. "He's in and out. I think he'll pull out of his coma soon. I've heard how much of a fighter he is."

Ramone dropped his head suddenly, shameful and a bit remorseful for causing the entire event to transpire. He wished he would've done things differently. "Damn. Yo, thanks for coming at that fat punk and all that. You didn't have to have my back like that, but you did. That's one hunnit, Shorty. Real shit."

"At the end of the day, this is Brooklyn. We all gotta stick together. I don't know why he comes all the way from Spanish Harlem to hustle on people. That's irritating." She rolled her eyes, but to Ramone, she looked so sexy.

Ramone held his rib cage and tried his best to sit upright better. "Yo, what's your Facebook. I wanna try to take you a somethin' when I come from under this whole ordeal. I gotta do something for you, nah mean."

She lowered her head and nodded. "ShaToya Miller. Send me a request, and we'll go from there." She leaned over him and got

closer. "I'm really sorry that you and your family have to go through this. You seem like a nice person."

Martha grew nauseous. She'd been at the hospital for twelve hours, and she needed a dope break. "Baby. I'll be back in a little while." She hugged herself. "I-I-I gotta go take care of something." She made her way to the door, glancing over her shoulder at him.

"Aiight, I'll see you then. Matter of fact, I'm good, ma. I'm sure Jayshawn will be, too. Gon' head, you're off the clock." Ramone fixed his pillow further behind him.

"Don't say it like that. I just got something I gotta do. I'll be back later." Martha slipped from the room. The doctor came toward her, ready to give her an update regarding Jayshawn. She held up her finger and kept going. "I just got something that I gotta do." She kept going.

Toya took Ramone's hand and looked into his eyes. "You sure you're okay?"

Before he could answer, two homicide detectives burst through the door with badges in their hands. "Ramone Stevens, we need to ask you some serious questions right now."

Chapter 5

Ramone folded his arms across his chest and refused to look the
lead Jewish investigative homicide detective in the eyes. "Yo, I'm
telling you right now, kid, I don't know shit about no murder. If
you're talking about that same fat muthafucka that got me laying
on this bed right now, you can really get the fuck outta this room.
Word up."

Charles Mason took his notepad out of his inside suit coat
pocket along with a blue pen. He was five feet nine inches, heavy
set, with milky skin, and heavily balding. "Look, kid, I don't
wanna have to go through this whole thing either, but as it stands,
the guy who shot you and your brother is laying on a slab
downtown with about fifty family members demanding justice.
It's either you talk to me now about who could have retaliated and
done this whole thing here, or I can book you in as a murder
suspect and have you moved downtown to the juvenile hall. It
doesn't really matter to me. I'm going home tonight, either way."

Ramone flared his nostrils. The streets of Brooklyn had long
ago taught him to never trust a policeman, and whenever you
encountered one, it'd be best to keep your mouth closed. Snitches
in Brooklyn were found cut up. And if their families were blessed
enough to find pieces of them that added up to a body, even then,
they weren't able to bury their dead relative because the funeral
would be shot up, or what the Shooters of the borough like to refer
to as a *drill*. Ramone wasn't risking any of that. "Yo, I don't know
what happened. The only thing I remember is this fat pedophile
standing over me after whooping my ass pretty bad with a gun.
My brother, Jayshawn, tried to get him up off of me. That's when
he popped him up, and then he turned the gun on me. Look, I just
turned sixteen yesterday. I'm just a kid. When I felt the slug enter
me, I closed my eyes and cried for my mother. That's my hand to
God."

Charles pursed his lips in disbelief. "I've been patrolling Red
Hook for over twenty years before I became a homicide detective.
One thing I never saw or heard of was a project kid hollering for

their mother once the heat was on," he scoffed. "So, I see what this is. You ain't gonna talk to the old pig, huh? Yeah, I figured as much. No big whoop as to why so many of your murders go unsolved in your neighborhoods; nobody wants to speak up. It seems like it's self-inflicted if you ask me. Oh well, whatta ya gonna do?"

Thomas Jones stood beside his partner with an angry scowl on his face. He was dark-skinned with beady eyes and a bald head. He stood six feet five inches tall and was muscle-bound with a big belly. He leaned over Ramone's bed. "Listen here, you dumb ass nigga. There is a dead man connected to yo black ass, and we ain't leaving this room until you tell us who the fuck did it. You see, my partner here he ain't familiar with dealing with you low-life scum bags, but I am. I got the same skin as you, but we ain't nothing alike." He placed his forehead on Ramone's. "Who did it?"'

Ramone jerked his head back. "Get ya sweaty ass head off of me. Fuck is yo problem, B?"

Thomas laughed maniacally. He grabbed hold of Ramone's neck and squeezed it as hard as he could with one hand and then two hands. "Who did it? Tell me! Tell you dumb ass bitch."

"Thomas! Thomas! Hey, stop it!" Charles Mason hollered, trying to pry his hands away from Ramone's throat.

Ramone's machines began to beep and go haywire. A short Black nurse ran into the room. When she saw what was taking place, she stopped in her tracks, and her eyes became bucked. "Oh my God! What are you two doing to him? Help! Help! They are killing this patient! Help!"

Charles grabbed her and tried to put his hand over her mouth. "Ma'am, please, shut up. I'm begging you!"

Twenty doctors and nurses ran into the room along with a security guard. Thomas released Ramone. Ramone saw the audience and decided to play into the scene. He convulsed and rolled out of bed, crying as loud as he could. The security guard called for backup as the nurses and doctors surrounded the detectives, guiding them out of the hospital and shaming them the entire time. But not before Thomas could threaten Ramone,

promising him he'd see him again and that when he did, the teen would be in major trouble. Ramone ignored him and cried louder. Toya knelt beside him, mugging the detectives as they left the hospital.

***

It was eight o'clock that night; the city had taken upon a cool breeze. The audio of police and ambulance sirens resonated all around the borough. Mosquitoes came out of their hiding places, looking for a delectable person to feast on. Jabari pulled his black-on-black Hellcat into the alley behind Coffey Park and stepped out of it dressed in all black Chanel from head to toe with a black fatigue Corona virus mask covering half of his face. He waited until his trusted young shooter got out of the passenger's seat of his whip before they walked a short path that led to a semi-truck that was parked just thirty feet away. Jabari balled his fist and beat on the trailer. He flipped his hoodie over his head and kept his head on a swivel. In Brooklyn, the war was on, and every second of every day, the Woos enemies were looking to catch them lacking by any means. Jabari refused to become a statistic.

The trailer rolled upward loudly in the night. Two Nigerian men stood in the entranceway with fully automatics in their hands. Jabari mugged them. "What's the deal, kid? We on or what?"

Sanka, the head Nigerian, knelt on one knee and shook up with Jabari before he took three steps back to allow him inside of the truck. "You were 'pose to come alone. Who is dis?" he asked him as both he and Travis stepped into the trailer.

"I could be asking you the same question regarding that ma-fucka that you're standing there with, but I ain't. You got your shooter, and I got mine, B. Let's get this shit on the road."

Sanka upped his silenced Glock .40, and before Jabari could react, he pressed it to a shocked Travis's head and pulled the trigger, knocking his brains out. "Clean it up."

Jabari jumped back, looking down at Travis in shock. "What the fuck you do that for?"

Two Nigerian women appeared out of the shadows. They snatched Travis out of the alley and threw it into a trunk that was already filled with plastic. They drove away with it. Two more women came with vicious pit bulls that ate up the pieces of brain that had been left behind. After the dogs had devoured all, they could find the area was doused in bleach, and that was that.

Sanka smacked his own chest. "We do things my way. You wanna be King of Brooklyn? You wanna eat with Nigeria? You listen, or we find a new King." Sanka upped a machete and placed the blade to Jabari's throat. "Ya understand me?"

Jabari lowered his eyes. "Yeah, I understand you real good too."

Sanka clenched his jaw and nodded at his henchmen. A black pillowcase was thrown over Jabari's head, and he was wrestled to the ground. His pockets were searched, and his car keys were removed. He felt a pinch in the side of his neck, and everything went black.

Chapter 6

When Jabari opened his eyes, there were two beautiful Black Barbie dolls looking down at him. Each woman smiled and looked at the other. They continued to fan him with huge colorful Peacock feathers. They were dressed in rich silks from Africa. Their hair was puffy and clean, full of sheen. Jabari sat up, and they knelt before him. He scooted back as far as he could inside of the gigantic golden throne that he had been placed on. Now that his eyes were opened, two more African female servants came to kneel before him. He looked around and noted that he was within a gorgeous palace. The walls were all white, with famous African art draped all over them. The chandeliers were pure gold, so were all of the statues that depicted African warriors. There were three fountains inside of the living room spewing the bluest water into a huge basin. Soft music churned from a distance. A beautiful teenage flutist sat crossed-legged on the floor playing a melody that warmed Jabari's heart. She was without a top.

Her beautiful perky early B cup breasts sat up on her chest with huge nipples that covered most of her globes. As she blew into her flute, dimples appeared upon each of her cheeks.

Sanka stepped into the room, holding a golden chalice that had black, green, and red diamonds all over it. He was also shirtless. His abs were deeply defined. His chest muscles flexed with each step that he took. "Ah-ha, Jabari, my brother, you are finally awake." He took a sip of his aged wine that had been sent to him from the jungles of the motherland.

Jabari stood up on wobbly legs. He braced himself and fell back into his chair. "What the fuck you give me, Sanka? I can't even see straight."

Sanka laughed as his long dreads fell past his waist. They were freshly twisted. "If you could see, you would understand that you are sitting in paradise. This is the ultimate goal." He knelt down and dug his hand into a duffel bag that was placed there. He pulled out a solid brick of gold and tossed it across the room to Jabari. Jabari tried to catch it, but his small motor skills had not

yet synched with the rest of himself. The gold bar hit his fingers and clanged to the floor. Jabari felt his head spinning. Sanka walked over and picked it up. He blew it off and handed it to him. "This is what royalty feels like."

Jabari looked over the bar for a moment before he tossed it back to Sanka. "What do you want from me?"

Sanka snapped his fingers. Suddenly two African Barbies appeared with a soft leather chair with gold around the edges of it. Sanka was about to take a seat when he caught himself. He nodded to Jabari. The women jumped up and helped Jabari to the newly presented chair while Sanka's throne was wiped off before he sat on it. Jabari tried once again to gain control of his senses. Sanka drank from his chalice once again. "Jabari, what I have in store for you is guaranteed to make you a very rich man. All I ask is for your complete cooperation. You do what I say and how I say it, no questions asked. You follow my directives and know that if ever you step outside of them that there will be consequences with no mercy. Do you understand that?"

Jabari wiped his nose and tried to swallow. There was not enough spit within his mouth to do so. He started to cough when a beautiful African Barbie appeared with a smaller chalice covered in diamonds. She guided the cup to his lips. He hesitated at first but then relented to the savory nectar. He groaned as he felt the juices restoring his mind and body. He drank all of the contents. When he finished, she wiped his mouth with a silk handkerchief and kissed his bare feet before disappearing into the back of the mansion. Jabari finally found his voice as two huge Lions slowly walked into the grand room and took a seat beside Sanka, one on each side of him.

"How are we going to go about this?" Jabari asked. He tightened his hands into fists, trying as best as he could to get some feeling back into them. The Barbies stood up and proceeded to fan him once again.

Sanka crossed his legs. "I was given word, from somebody you don't really need to know right now, to choose you to take

over New York City." He sipped his cup and paused for a Barbie to wipe his lips.

Jabari flared his nostrils. "Before anything, I'm a mutha-fuckin' jack boy. All I know is murder and guns. I don't know what the fuck you think you're about to have me doing, but it's gon' take some time before I'm ready to take over a whole muthafuckin' city. I'm used to running behind Paperchase and letting him do everything while I clean up his dirty work. Who the fuck is choosing me for this shit right here? I wanna know."

Sanka shook his head. "In time, but just to give you a sense of clues. What are you?"

"I'm Woo. A Brooklyn shooter. Drill shit. That's all I know."

Sanka sighed. "I'm not talking about some low-life gang that, when it all boils down, can be wiped off of the face of the earth with very little effort. No, what is your nationality? What are your parents?"

"I don't know my pops, but my mother is Nigerian. Full-blooded. She said my old man was too, but that's her story to tell, not mine. I ain't never met the nigga."

"Don't use that word ever again, do you understand me? It's a word of ignorance and idiocy. If I ever hear you say it toward me again, there will be extreme consequences." Sanka's heart pounded in his chest.

"Yo, my bad, dawg. I get it." Jabari looked up to the Barbies that were fanning him. They smiled at him and grew serious again. "Yo, what my nationality gotta do with anything?"

"It's everything. Your roots are important for the next endeavors that you are about to enter into. But it all starts with the dismantling of Brooklyn."

Jabari stood up. "What? Never. I am Brooklyn, B. I'd never switch sides. Brooklyn is the epicenter of the world."

Sanka laughed, "are you done?"

Jabari mugged him. "Yeah, I guess. Fuck, you got against Brooklyn, Dunn? We don't fuck with nobody that ain't fucking with us. Word to the borough."

Sanka shook his head. "Sit yo dumb, ghetto, no class having ass down before I pierce you with a spear and try this again with somebody else." A Barbie handed him a long stick with a golden spear on the end of it. It gleamed in the palace.

Jabari sat down. "Why the fuck are you always threatening me, huh? Is this going to be the extent of our relationship because if so, this shit ain't gon' end well?"

Sanka smiled. "Jabari, you said one thing right. And that's Brooklyn is the epicenter of the world, especially when it comes to narcotics. If you are looking to destroy, divide, and conquer New York, it must start in Brooklyn. As we know, New York is the nucleus of the United States of America. However, your job is basic. I am going to supply you with everything that you need to infect and destroy the inner city of Brooklyn. I'm talking guns, drugs, pills, codeine, everything. And in exchange for you doing so, I will make sure you become a very rich and powerful King."

Jabari rubbed his chin. "So, you're telling me as long as I flood the streets with dope, you'll make sure I become what every mafucka struggling in the trenches wanna become? Is that it?"

Sanka nodded, "That's it."

Jabari wasn't buying it, "what's the catch?"

"No, catch if your true goal in life is to become royalty. Look at this shit here. Just look around. This palace is yours. The women, the gold, the cars within the underground parking, all of it is yours. All I need from you is two years of service, and you'll see what I do."

Jabari stood up. "With positions like this, them bitchez bring hella enemies. Who the fuck I gotta war with?"

"Everybody. You will officially become the most hated, most envied, number one target by the Feds and the hungry animals that seek to devour in the trenches."

Jabari waved it off. "That's been the case all along. I don't give any fucks about that. As long as I got my Woo niggaz, I mean my Woo homies, my bad, I ain't worried about shit."

Sanka was quiet. "About that. You see, with every new position comes a great sacrifice. Your position is no different. We

demand three sacrifices. We choose, of course, all three, but the first will be very simple."

This was starting to become weird to Jabari. He stared at Sanka, confused. "Fuck is the first one?"

Sanka stood up, and his lions did as well. He walked to the patio balcony that overlooked the ocean. The harsh waves crashed into each over before they were still. His shooters canvassed the area on both boats and jet skis. Their pitch-black skin looked beautiful in the sunlight. "Paperchase."

Jabari closed his eyes. "Fuck that, why him?"

Sanka continued to look off into the distance as the scene played before his mind's eye. It was an early Saturday morning in Harlem, New York. Sankeesy was just finishing up sweeping the entire bodega before she opened the doors ready for service when a masked Scorpion and two of his Jack boys rushed into her store and took a hold of her. Scorpion took it upon himself to rough her up pretty good before he threw her to the floor and tied her up with duct tape while his men ransacked the store.

Sankeesy got up while Scorpion had his back turned and attacked him from behind. Well versed in the art of combat, she jumped into the air and kicked him in the middle of the back, crippling him to his knees. She went on the attack against the remaining men but was soon outdone. They had gotten the better of her. By the time Scorpion made it to his feet, she was bound with a gun to her head. The shooter looked up to Scorpion and asked him if he should pull the trigger. Scorpion debated for a minute before he muffed Sankeesy to the floor and ordered his men to flee with no further harm done to her.

Over the years, this had been the only reason for Sanka having not crushed Scorpion and his outfit already. That, and Sankeesy had begged him for mercy for the sake of Scorpion because, in her mind, he had saved her life. Sanka promised never to lay a finger on him, but it didn't stop him from slaying the remainder of the men that were present during the robbery. He'd gutted them like fish and fed their still warm hearts to his lions that were only cubs

back then. And though it had been more than ten years ago, Sanka remembered the day like it was yesterday.

He came back to the present. "Your first sacrifice is Paperchase. You have three months, and so it begins."

Chapter 7

Olivia sat cross-legged in the bed across from Paperchase looking into his bright brown eyes. She took hold of the sides of his face and leaned her forehead into his. She made a low-pitched humming sound. There were candles lit all around them, and a soft meditating song coming from the speakers decorated in each upper corner of the room. Olivia continued to hum.

Paperchase jerked his head back after allowing her to do that for the straight ten minutes. He could feel his phone vibrating, and the constant notice of it was throwing him off. He scooted backward and stood up on the side of the bed. Olivia frowned and lowered her head in frustration.

"Yo, I'm sorry, boo. I'm trying like a muthafucka, but I just can't seem to get jiggy with this shit. You don't really want me to do it no way."

Olivia stepped out of bed on pretty toes and took hold of his hands. "It's not that I don't necessarily want you to, but to have you with me upon this journey to inner peace would be nice. All this killing and all of the souls that I feel are chasing us always tend to go away after I meditate."

"Yeah, well, I don't really believe in any of that shit. I be trying, but it just don't work for me as much as I wish it would." He broke away from her and popped two Xanax along with a Percocet Thirty. He chased it with a thick dosage of Lean.

Olivia stepped around to him. "Because that's what you turn to whenever this life begins to get the better of you. Those fuckin' drugs. Why don't you ever talk to me about how you really feel when it comes to all of this shit that we're faced with, huh? When will all of the killing stop? When will we tell Scorpion that we want to be together? When will you walk away from the Woo so that we can raise a family? What are you waiting on?"

Paperchase mugged her from the corners of his eyes. "I ain't never said nothing about leaving the Woo. And what's with all of this family talk? I don't even know what that shit looks like. You already know I'ma street nigga, word the fuck up."

Olivia shook her head. "That street shit ain't gonna lead neither one of us nowhere but dead or locked down like your brother." She sighed loudly, "I gotta be honest, I don't know if I wanna do this next job. I mean, where is it going to get us anyway? What, killing people is going to get Scorpion home, how so? He still ain't told us about that side of the coin just yet."

Paperchase rested his hands on the dresser and lowered his head. "Look, I don't know what's all of this boiling down to, but we have to trust the process. My brother ain't never steered me wrong ever since I was a little boy. I don't know what he got us his sleeve, but I'm telling you that it'll all be worth it in the end."

"In the end? Maurice, do you hear yourself? I mean, really, do you?"

"Yeah, I do. What the fuck kind of question is that?" He snapped, feeling the Percocet starting to kick into his system. His body got hot then itchy. He looked at her, feeling high as a kite.

"Do you know what that looks like, you know, with him being free and all? What does it look like for us? I mean, I don't even know what that looks like, but all I know is that I love you with all of my heart and soul. Maurice, I will die for you. Most of the things I do aren't for Scorpion. They are for you. You are my life, ever since you saved me from him taking it away from me."

Though Scorpion loved Olivia dearly, he had always been an extremely jealous man. All it would take was for another man to lay eyes on Olivia or for her to respond to an admirer in a way that Scorpion found disrespectful, and he'd beat her senseless, all the while explaining to her why he was doing so. One time he'd been dead set on beating Olivia to death until Paperchase had stepped in and talked sense into him after pulling him off of her. Olivia remembered the day like it was yesterday, and so did Paperchase.

"So, tell me, Maurice. If Scorpion is released, what happens to us? I want to know the truth."

Paperchase beamed. He was so high that he couldn't even think straight. "Yo, I don't wanna talk about any of that shit right now. We're going to keep doing what the fuck bro says and see this shit through. When we get to the end of the mission, all of that

other shit will be revealed to us and not before then. Take yo' ass in there and get ready. We gotta be out of here by eight tonight."

Olivia stomped her foot. "I'm not doing this shit for him anymore! I'm not, but if you want me to keep on risking my life in these streets, then I will. Just tell me that you love me and that no matter what, in the end, it's going to be you and me." She walked over to him and wrapped her arms around his neck. "Please, Papi."

Paperchase waited for a moment before he looked into her almond-shaped eyes. He brought his forehead to hers. It will be, boo. That, I promise you. You're my baby girl. I don't give a fuck if you are a little older than me." He kissed her lips. It was time for them to perform their next mission.

***

Annnnnnnnn! Clank! The prison cell door slid to the right. Scorpion waited until it was all the way opened before he stepped through it. He adjusted his socks, rolling them all of the way up. Tucked safely inside of it was a sharpened nine-inch nail that had been made into a deadly shank. He had two sharpened shanks made out of metal along his waist, and his chest was covered with magazines that were used as a prison bulletproof vest. Though bullets were hardly the worry, this vest was used to protect him from other shanks of the ops that roamed around the prison looking to knock off the Brooklyn chapter's leader of the Woo.

Scorpion walked down the gallery of prison cells, cautious with his head on a swivel. Each cell that he passed, he made sure that there weren't any occupants inside of it before he strolled on his way. His hand remained clutched around the shank on his right side, which was also his dominant hand. After clearing the row of cells, he departed from the cell house and wound up in the huge main laundry portion of the prison. Inside of it, there was the leader of the Haitians out of Queens. The short, dark-skinned man referred to as Hoffa met him with a handshake.

"Peace, brother," Hoffa said this and hugged Scorpion. They touched each other's shoulders with their chin three times. Both men were Muslim, and this was their customary greeting.

"Peace." Scorpion led Hoffa into the back of the laundry room, where all of the dryers were. "This District Attorney is the biggest thorn in your side, am I right?"

Hoffa nodded, "the whole reason why I'm guaranteeing you what I am. If you get rid of this muthafucka for me, I'll give you the information on where three political bodies are buried. Remember that white girl that went missing six months ago that is still all over the news? Or the couple that disappeared from out of Staten Island? The father was worth $500,000,000?"

"Yeah, Akki, I remember both of those cases."' Scorpion assured him. "You got the skinny?"

"You already know. You do your part, and I'll be sure to do mine. Those three unsolved murders will get you home quicker than you can say fuck Nigeria." He laughed. It was no secret that the Nigerians and Haitians hated each other with a passion for reasons unknown to anybody other than the pair of nationalities.

"You got my word that this shit will be taken care of tonight. I got this. You handle yo' end, and it's official. Peace and blessing." He hugged him again, and Hoffa kissed him on the cheek, and then Scorpion was gone.

Chapter 8

Olivia ran her French manicured fingers through her curly hair and took a sip from the expensive champagne once again. She felt nervous, and on top of that, she had a migraine that was causing her vision to go blurry ever so often. She took a deep breath and tried to calm her spirit. She closed her eyes as Blake Kavanaugh came beside her and looked her up and down. Olivia smiled and sipped her drink. Soft jazz music played from a live band up on the stage. The ballroom was full of the upper crust of New York sporting their most expensive attire. Olivia's cream and white Vera Wang gown had been a ten-thousand-dollar investment. She made sure that she kept the tag tucked and that perfume had only been sprayed along the sides of her neck and wrists.

Blake stood a little closer. "When I ordered an escort from the agency, I didn't realize that they would respect me enough to send the most beautiful one that they had. Label me honored." He held up his crystal champagne glass and saluted her before taking a drink.

"Well, I don't know if I should take that statement as a compliment or an insult because you see I am not an escort. I am here by happenstance." Olivia thought about the skinny white escort that Paperchase had caught snorting a line of Meth in her Miata before he snatched her up and trapped her within the trunk of his car. Olivia smiled and batted her eyelashes at him.

"Oh my God. I have never been more embarrassed in my life. Please forgive me; it's just that everyone here is paired up with the exception of you. You're waiting by the bar looking oh so scrumptious, and I just thought..."

"...That a Puerto Rican and Black girl with so many curves must be selling her twat to the highest bidder?" she scoffed. "I'll have you know that I am worth five hundred million dollars. I am a cosmetic line guru. When it's all said and done, Maybelline will be kissing that tush that you've been ogling ever since you stepped into this little soirée."

"Ahhhh, so you did notice me walking into this little shindig, huh? I guess I'm not the only one scoping the scene, looking for a prospect." He leaned into her.

Olivia smirked, "prospect? That a new word for ass or what?" She giggled and took a sip from her champagne. "Later, big shot."

Blake watched her switch her hips through the crowd of uppity people. He felt a stirring deep within his loins, one of which he hadn't felt in thirty years. He ran his hand over his graying black silky hair and headed after her. "Excuse me, miss, I didn't catch your name." He caught up to her at the exit.

"That's because I never gave it to you." She checked the time on her Audemars Piguet.

Blake felt fidgety. He didn't understand how Olivia was having such an effect on him. Maybe it was her sexy accent. Maybe it was the scent of her. Maybe it was her curves that seemed endless, or maybe it was because she was the most beautiful woman that he had ever seen in all of his life. Whatever the reason, he had to have her. "If I may, madam, I don't know who you are or where you came from, but I promise to give you whatever you want. I mean, I will lay it at your perfect feet if only you would spend a night with me. I promise to make it worth more than your while. What do you say, huh?"

Olivia looked him up and down from the side of her face. "I have never been more insulted...," She started to walk away. He dropped his head in defeat. "And yet, intrigued at the same time. Howsa 'bout you walk me to my car? A big strapping man like you could so easily protect me."

Blake bowed his head. "I would be ever so delighted, my lady."

Olivia curtsied. "Then right this way."

They were halfway out into the dark parking lot with Blake talking a mile a minute when Paperchase appeared behind him. Olivia caught sight of Paperchase from the corners of her eyes, and she kept walking. By the time Blake noticed Paperchase, he was placing a taser into the back of his neck and shocking him into a paralyzed state. Blake dropped to the ground, and Olivia popped

the trunk of her red Bentley. He stole a glance at her watch and looked back up at Paperchase. "Look, tonight is girls' night out. I need to get home, shower, and get dressed. So, you think you can have one of your guys help you with this lil' task?"

"Yeah, I'ma scoop up my nigga Goo."

"That short, chubby, dark-skinned nigga with the mouthful of gold?"

"Yeah. That's him. Man, this nigga heavy as fuck, yo!" Paperchase complained as he hoisted Blake up over his shoulders. He dumped him into the trunk of the Bentley. Olivia slammed the trunk shut and smacked imaginary dirt from her hands. When she looked to Paperchase, he was hunched over with his hands on his knees. His face was shiny from sweat, and he was breathing hard. Blake's ass was far heavier than he looked.

"Okay, look, I'm dropping you off at the house, snatch up Goo, then I'm taking this cracka ass cracka to Brooklyn ASAP. I'll hit up big bruh and see where he wants us to take it from there."

"That's one of the many qualities I love about you, baby. You're a natural-born leader." Olivia puckered up for a kiss and took a step forward. Paperchase gave a cautious look around to make sure there wasn't anyone that knew them watching him before he kissed her. "Come on, big poppa, let's roll."

***

Ramone had been out of the hospital for a week when one morning, on his way to the corner bodega Jabari pulled his black-on-black Charger up beside him as he was crossing the street. Jabari beeped the horn twice until Ramone stopped. Jabari rolled down the window and stuck his head out of it. "Get yo lil' ass in the car so I can holler at you, Slime."

Ramone didn't hesitate. He opened the passenger's door and got inside. As soon as his feet hit the mats, Jabari pulled off. Ramone rested his arm on the seal of the window. "So, what's good?'

Jabari mugged him. "I know the police been up yo ass over that dead fat nigga, haven't they?"

Ramone nodded, thinking about the way the two detectives had hemmed him up at the hospital. "Yeah, they worked me over and all of that. I stayed solid, though. Fuck Twelve, on gang."

Jabari laughed, "On gang? Boy, what the fuck does that mean?"

Ramone suddenly felt embarrassed. "It's just a thing we say. It don't mean nothing, really." He looked out of the window and saw that they were getting on the highway. "Yo Dunn, where the fuck we going, B?"

"Calm ya nerves, kid. It's good. You cruising wit' a boss right now. That's all the fuck you need to know. Sit yo' lil' ass back."

Ramone frowned and shook his head, sitting back like he was ordered. "Where are we rolling, too, though? The reason I ask is because my brother came out of his coma a few days ago, and I finally got enough chump change to catch the train there and back to go and see him. I gotta be there to support him, nah mean? That fat nigga could have slumped him."

Jabari understood, "Yeah, I get it, B. I'll make sure that you get to him in time. But exactly at what time is that, though?"

"About five, that'll be perfect." Ramone saw that Jabari had a bag of McDonald's. His stomach growled so loud that Jabari heard it.

Jabari tossed him the bag. "It's a couple of Big Macs in there kid, they're yours."

"Nah, I don't eat off other people and shit. I got good home training." Ramone's stomach growled again.

"Yeah, aight. Fuck it, den. I'll just toss this shit; it is what it is." He grabbed the bag and rolled down his window to call Ramone's bluff.

Ramone snatched the bag. "You wildin' son, I'd never let you do that." He grabbed the Big Mac and started tearing into it with no remorse.

"Yo, what ya home life looking like, kid? No cap, either."

"We fucked up just like every other family in Red Hook. My moms is strung out on that needle and all that. We got more roaches than food, but what ya gonna do. It's all I know. The struggle is real, word." He stuffed a bunch of French fries into his mouth.

Jabari felt sick on the stomach. "I think you keeping yo' mouth closed when those pigs came to holler at you was real nigga shit. On my Woo, ain't too many solid lil' niggaz like that no more in Buck Town. I got something for you." He dug in his pocket and handed him a five-thousand-dollar knot of cash that he'd gotten dropped off from one of his workers. "That's five bands, nigga, on Woo. I don't care what the fuck you do wit' it, but if you were smart, you'd take care of your home situation. Keep those blue faces from ya moms, word to Jehovah. If she gets a hold of those joints ya ass gon' be sad as fuck."

Ramone talked with his mouth full, "I ain't no dummy. I don't know how I can repay you. Maybe I can drill somebody for you. I don't care who it is." Ramone was spitting food all over his lap because his mouth was so full.

Jabari smacked his lips. "Blood, what you know about drilling?"

"I'm from Brooklyn, son. That's all it is out here, word to the borough. But that's neither here nor there." H held up one finger and took a swallow of the Pepsi. He burped. "I got potnas out in Queens that are already drilling for their big homies. They get paid that stupid gwop. I'm tryna get down too. That Woo shit is in my heart already. The Woo is Red Hook."

Jabari didn't understand why but Ramone was really tugging on his heartstrings. "Yo, I tell you what lil' homie. I'ma send you through a few tests to see what that heart looks like inside of your chest, and we'll go from there. Until then, you stay close to me, and I'ma make sure you eat. Every street nigga adopts a young homie. Well, consider yourself adopted. I'm about to turn yo ass into a pure demon. The opps won't even see you coming." Jabari smiled wickedly. "Come on, let's go visit your brother."

Chapter 9

Ramone and Jabari walked inside Jayshawn's room to find him awake. He was lying in bed looking at the television set mounted on the wall. His eyes were narrow, and his lips were partially open. He was wearing a blue and white gown. An IV was in the vein at the top of his right hand, and his hospital bracelet was around his left wrist. Seeing movement at the corner of his eye, Jayshawn looked to his door and saw his brother and Jabari approaching. The brothers smiled at each other as soon as they laid eyes on one another. Ramone rushed to his brother's side and hugged him.

"Oooooh!" Jayshawn winced in pain.

"My bad, yo, I forgot chu had been shot," Ramone said by way of an apology.

"Shit, me too until you came and hugged me." Jayshawn cracked a grin. "I love and miss you, baby brother."

"I love and missed you too, big bro," Ramone replied, shaking up with him. Jayshawn grabbed him by the back of his neck, pulled him close, and pressed his forehead against his. They both shut their eyes while he recited a prayer and thanked the Lord for watching over Ramone since he'd been out of commission.

"Amen," Jayshawn said at the same time Ramone did. He then kissed his little brother on the side of his head and released him. "Who that over there, son?" he looked around Ramone and saw Jabari walking over to him. They slapped hands and shook up.

"What up, Dunn? How you feeling?" Jabari smirked.

"High as a kite," Jayshawn smiled goofily. "That morphine is a mothafucka, son. One minute I was in pain, and the next, I'm floating on cloud nine. Did you know heroin was made from this shit, yo? Now, how the fuck do these white folks get the FDA to approve this shit?"

"The world will never know, my G," Jabari told him.

"Anyway, what you and baby bro been up to?" Jayshawn inquired, looking back and forth at them.

"Shit, really. I scooped the young homie up, he ate some Mickey D's, and decided to come up here to see big bro." Jabari grinned and tapped him on his leg. He pulled up the chair that Ramone had just given him and sat down. Ramone grabbed another chair and sat down on the opposite side of him.

"Y'all niggaz cold as a hooka's heart. How y'all not gon' bring the kid back nothing?" Jayshawn said playfully.

"Word is bond, yo, you two niggaz ain't shit. Y'all know this food up here is as nasty as them stripper bitchez that be dancing up at Show Palace." Jabari and Ramone laughed and exchanged glances.

"Yo, I could go grab you a bite to eat down in the hospital cafeteria," Ramone told him. "They got all kinda shit down there. I saw this white dude with some Buffalo wings and French fries with Ranch dressing. I know you fucks with that."

"Bet."

"Okay." Ramone hopped up from his chair and made his way for the door. He turned around when his big brother called him back.

"Bring me back a strawberry Fanta, my guy—with just a lil' ice."

"Aiight. I got chu," Ramone assured him before he disappeared through the door.

"Damn, I forgot to give him some money," Jayshawn said to no one in particular.

"Don't worry about it. I laid a couple of dollars on him."

Jayshawn frowned when he said this. "Oh, yeah? For what exactly?" He winced as he sat up in bed. He pressed a button on a handheld device that fed more morphine to his bloodstream.

"Couple of dicks hemmed him up asking questions, and my son held it down," Jabari told him. "Me and mine appreciate that, so I had to bless the youngin', nah mean?"

Jayshawn nodded with understanding while staring ahead. He then focused his attention back on him. "Yo, Jabari, how long you figure we've been knowing each other?"

Jabari scratched his temple while staring out the corners of his eyes. "Shiiiiit, I'd say since, uhhhh, elementary."

"That's right, since Brooklyn Gardens, Mrs. Odom's class," Jayshawn reminded him. "I got wild love and respect for you." He tapped his fist to his chest.

Jabari adjusted himself in his chair and leaned forward. He had a serious look on his face now. "I can say the same. But what are you getting at, Slime? What you trying to say?"

"Look, bro, you and I are as cool as a fan, but I'd appreciate it if you leave baby bro alone. I know how you and Paperchase get down and the kinda business y'all are mixed up in. I don't want my lil' man getting mixed up in that. You feel me?"

"Bro, where do you get off telling me what the fuck to do? Ramone is only sixteen, but we both know in the hood that's considered a grown-ass man," Jabari told him like it is. "I love the kid, and I fucks with bro. As far as I can see, the lil' homie is solid. I'm never gon' turn my back on him."

"Ramone is my lil' brother. He is my concern! I'ma take care of him!" Jayshawn raised his voice, jabbing his finger at his chest.

"Take care of him? Nigga, are you serious?" Jabari smiled and licked his lips. "Big bro, if you were taking care of the youngin', he wouldn't have been out here in these streets starving, resorting to stealing hot dogs and shit."

"Yo, my nigga, word to everything I love, stay the fuck away from my lil' man," Jayshawn spat angrily. His being pissed off had begun to sober him up. If it wasn't for his wounds having left him in such a weakened state, he would have mopped the floor with Jabari's ass.

"Fuck you gon' do if I don't, nigga?" Jabari fired back. He wanted to blow Jayshawn's brains out, but he forgot he'd left his gun behind in his car. He couldn't get it inside of the hospital through the metal detector, and he thought that was a good thing. He was a trigger-happy nigga, and he was sure he would have murdered Jayshawn in the presence of the medical staff.

Jayshawn sat there staring at Jabari in silence as he mean mugged him. He knew how the boy gave it up. He was nasty with

the gunplay, and word around the borough was he'd killed more niggaz than cancer. Jayshawn, on the other hand, had a wicked knuckle game. He was skilled in martial arts called 52 Blocks, often referred to as Jailhouse Rock. He learned this style of fighting during his time in prison for strong-arm robbery. The technique was said to have been developed hundreds of years ago by African slaves. Their masters would take them around to different plantations to bare-knuckle brawl with the slaves of other masters for money. Still, fighting and killing were two different things. A man may have the nerve to throw down, but that doesn't mean he had it in him to take someone's life.

Jayshawn knew without a shadow of a doubt if he bumped heads with Jabari, it would most definitely end in bloodshed. And he was more than willing to take it there. He loved his brother enough to kill for him, as well as die for him, that he was sure of.

"I'm not one to make threats, so cross the line and find out for yo damn self," Jayshawn told him, with menacing eyes and flaring nostrils. His fists were balled so tight the veins in them were bulging.

"Oh, yeah? That's yo word?" Jabari hopped out of his chair with his fists at his sides.

"Nigga, that's my word," Jayshawn spat back. He was as hot as fish grease and ready to get it popping, fresh gunshot wounds and all. Unbeknownst to Jabari, he slipped his left hand underneath his thigh and grasped a dinner fork. He kept it from the meal he'd eaten earlier before him and Ramone's arrival. He didn't know who Fat Juan was connected to, and it was possible his people would come looking for some get-back. Although the fork wasn't a gun, he'd rather have it than nothing at all should a hundred Spanish niggaz rushed his room looking for blood.

Jabari was about to make his move on Jayshawn until Ramone bobbed back into the room, popping a French fry in his mouth.

"Aye, bro, I hope you don't mind, but I ate a couple of your—" the words died in Ramone's throat when he noticed the hostile expressions on his brother and Jabari's faces. He sat the clear

container of food on the rolling table beside his brother's bed. "Yo, what the fuck is up? What's poppin' with y'all?"

"Ain't shit, just a lil' dispute over the game, don't worry about it," Jabari told him. "But check it, my dude, I'ma let you rock with ya fam while I chill out in the car. I need to chief one." He slapped hands with Ramone and shook up with him. He cast a look that could kill over his shoulder at Jayshawn as he made his way towards the door. 'Fuck you,' Jayshawn mouthed at him when Ramone turned to pull up his chair. Jabari threw up two middle fingers as he walked backwards.

Ramone glanced over his shoulder, and Jabari switched up. He pretended to be smiling and waving goodbye. Ramone looked up at the television set mounted on the wall. An episode of *Love & Hip-Hop Atlanta* was playing. Frowning, he focused his attention on Jayshawn.

"Yo, y'all niggaz wasn't arguing over no fucking game, cut the shit! The TV isn't even on the right channel for that, so what's really good?" Ramone asked.

Jayshawn took a breath. "I don't want you running the streets with that nigga Jabari. He's bad news."

"What are you talking about, bro? That's my nigga. Son looks out for me."

"Yeah, he told me about them few dollars he hit yo hand with," Jayshawn replied. "That nigga ain't slick, though. He's enticing you with that dough, so you'll be more inclined to do dirt for him to get more of it."

"On some real shit, bro, I don't care. I'm trying to level up," Ramone said with serious eyes. "And if it means selling my soul to the Devil, I'm ready and willing to putta price tag on it. You feel me? I'm not gon' wait and let our family die so they can get to Heaven. Fuck that! I'ma do whatever I have to do in my power to make sure I create a Heaven, right here on this earth." He emphasized by jabbing his finger at the floor. Tears descended his cheeks, and he wiped them away quickly.

Jayshawn sniffled and wiped away his as well. He couldn't help feeling like he'd failed to take care of his brother. He made an

honest living cutting dope boys' hair in the projects, mowing lawns, recycling, hustling weed, and working for the Puerto Ricans at the bodega. Still, that money wasn't nearly enough to take care of cloth, feed, and buy all of the necessities his younger brother needed. He'd been taken on the burden of running a household since before he was old enough to buy alcohol. He didn't have a choice since their mother was strung out on dope, and their Pops had left them to fend for themselves.

Jayshawn felt like shit at the bottom of someone's heel thinking about the circumstances he was raising his brother in. He knew he could have made their lives a lot easier by selling drugs, but he refused to slang the same poison his mother was dependent on to someone else's mother. That would put another family in the same fucked up position that he and his loved ones were in, and he couldn't live with that, but clearly, Ramone's mind could deal with the weight of that burden. The thought of his brother being so selfish and heartless broke his heart. But he understood where the young nigga was coming from. He was sick and tired of struggling and being poor. And now, he was willing to do whatever he had to do to change their lives for the better.

"I'm—I'm sorry, man. I am truly, truly sorry," Jayshawn's voice cracked emotionally. He hardly ever showed his vulnerable side to his younger brother. But it was him who he felt most comfortable showing this side of him to.

Ramone's forehead wrinkled. He didn't know what his big brother was talking about. "What are you talking about, bro? What're you sorry for?"

Jayshawn looked away, swallowing his spit. He looked Ramone in his eyes. "I'm sorry for how you came up. I'm sorry for ma, pops, growing up poor as shit. Lil' bro, I'm sorry for failing you as a brother and a par—"

"Nah," Ramone shook his head. "You didn't have anything to do with who we were born to or how I grew up. This was the hand we were dealt," he assured him. "You didn't fail me as a brother or a parent. You got us this far by doing nearly everything by the

book. Well, I'ma take it from here and do things my way. And I'ma get us out of The Bricks. I promise."

Ramone pulled out what was left of the five bandz after paying for Jayshawn's meal. He tried to give him half of it, but he refused to take it.

"Nah, baby bro, I can't take that. That's yours," Jayshawn told him.

"You're my big bruh; whatever is mine is half yours, always," Ramone told him. Jayshawn reluctantly took the money. He pulled his sibling into him and hugged him with his good arm. He rested his head against the side of his and kissed him on the side of the face.

"I love you, Ramone," Jayshawn said, teary-eyed.

Ramone's closed his eyes to suppress his tears, but they came anyway. "I love you, even more, big bruh. And don't worry about nothing, from here on out, I got us." He shook up with him and headed for the door wiping his tears away.

Jayshawn wiped his tears away, snorted, and licked his lips. "Yo, Ramone!"

Ramone gathered his wits and took a deep breath. He looked to his brother with a halfhearted grin. "Tell that nigga Jabari I meant what I said, yo."

Ramone frowned, wondering what his brother was talking about. He knew without a doubt he wouldn't tell him if he asked, so he just nodded and went about his business.

Chapter 10

"Take a look around you, Slime. Take a real good look, and tell me what you see," Jabari told Ramone, with a fat ass blunt pinched between his finger and thumb. The young nigga was taking in the streets from the passenger seat.

"I see home. I see Brooklyn, yo," Ramone answered and then looked over at him.

"That's right. And it's all mine," Jabari assured him before passing him the blunt. "I'm about to make a few moves that's gon' have me sitting on the throne. I'm finna be the king of all this shit." Ramone listened closely while smoking the blunt. "I'ma take the whole shit over, no cap, but I'll need you and a dozen or so young demons like you if I'm gonna do it, ya heard?"

Ramone nodded and said, "Yeah, I feel you."

"We're gonna have to knock a few heads off to show niggaz out here we're not playing, B," Jabari told him as he took the blunt back. By this time, Ramone's eyes were red and glassy, and he was slumped down in the seat. He slipped the hood of his hoodie over his head and continued to stare out of the window as Jabari gave his lecture. "Mothafuckaz gon' only have two choices Blood, either bow down to something greater than themselves or eat a clip full of some hot shit. My word to God."

"No doubt," Ramone replied lazily, feeling the effects of the Kush.

"I want you to be my top gunna, son, my number one goon," Jabari confessed. He looked over at him to see his reaction. "All you gotta do is stay loyal and knock down any nigga that gets in the way of our rise to power. If you can do that, I promise I'll make you rich beyond your wildest dreams. You will be able to move outta The Bricks into your own lil' spot. And you'll never have to worry about going hungry again. You've just gotta pass these lil' tests I got set up for you and pledge yo' allegiance to a nigga. You good with that?"

"A nigga starving out here, son. No lie," Ramone began. "I don't give a fuck who I gotta crush in order for me and mine to

eat. Just gimme a strap, point the nigga out, and I'ma eat his food, word to the Gods."

"I hear you talking, my young nigga."

The Dodge Charger zipped up the street, with its Hemi engine whining like an old muscle car, alerting all within a twenty-block radius to its presence. Jabari was going well over the speed limit, with some very heavy weaponry on board, but he didn't give a fuck about getting pulled over. Maybe it was the weed or the promising future that lay ahead with Sanka, but this night he felt invincible, like nothing or no one in the world could touch him.

The full moon shone on the windshield of Jabari's whip when he stopped at a red traffic light. Bobbing his head, he spat the lyrics to Casanova's *So Brooklyn*. Suddenly a woman's screaming and hollering rang out, garnering him and Ramone's attention. They looked over their shoulders out of the passenger window to find a dark-caramel skinned man with waist-length dreadlocks. He had his hand wrapped around a woman's neck, shaking her furiously while a younger woman was trying to pull him off her. Two more men stood at his back, doubled over, laughing and pointing.

"Get the fuck off me!" the man with the waist-length dread-locks barked at the younger woman holding his arm. He yanked free of her, and backhand slapped her. She spun around like a ballerina and hit the sidewalk.

"Yo, son, ain't that Toya and ya moms?" Jabari narrowed his eyes as he looked through the window.

"Hell yeah!" Ramone said, setting his book aside and unbuck-ling his safety belt.

"What the fuck they do to piss off that nigga?" Jabari asked no one in particular.

"I don't know, and I don't give a damn! Nigga fucked up put-ting his paws on mine!" Ramone hopped out of the car and slammed the door behind him. He took off running towards the action while that nigga Jabari sped off to find someplace to park.

"Ack, ack, ack, ack, ack!" Martha gagged with watery eyes as the nigga rocking the dreadlocks clenched her by the neck. His

grip was iron, and there were veins running up and down his muscular arm. Martha gasped for air, struggling to breathe while she punched and kicked at him.

Toya lay on the sidewalk, dazed and confused with a redden cheek. She tried to get up, but her equilibrium was off.

"Bitch, you've got some goddamn nerve askin' the God to fill yo' prescription when you haven't even paid me for the last time I got you right," Shakur The God spat angrily with venom dripping from his vocal cords. He had a goatee, and his waist-length dreadlocks were twisted tight and greasy. At twenty-eight years old, he stood six-foot-one and weighed every bit of 230 pounds of all muscle. He sported a black eye patch over his left eye with a gold seven-point, Five Percenter Star on it, and the number 7 at the center of the star. The gold twinkled like diamond dust beneath the streetlights.

"You know about me and how I give it up. It ain't no secret." He pulled his .44 Magnum Revolver from the small of his back and cocked it with his thumb. He pressed its barrel below her left eye indented her cheek. "That means you know what comes with playing with the God's gwop."

Shakur The God was about to blow Martha's brains out when one of his flunkies shouted a warning to him. When he looked over his shoulder, Ramone was flying at him with a kick. Shakur The God dropped his gun and went hurling through the large front window of the Chinese take-out joint. He knocked over a table and a couple of chairs as he slid across the floor along with pieces of broken glass.

There were small bloody cuts scattered over his face and neck. Looking up, he groaned and shook the broken glass from his dreadlocks. He scowled and clenched his jaws when he saw Ramone helping his mother to her feet while she coughed and massaged her sore neck. He then ran over to Toya and held her at the shoulders, taking stock of the damage done to her.

A Chinese man and woman ran from behind the bulletproof glass, unlocked the door, and ran out onto the floor. The woman

held the man's arm while he hurled shit in his native language and wagged his cordless telephone at Shakur The God.

"I call the police now, take everyone ass jail!" the Chinese man swore and did just that.

Shakur The God rose from the floor with broken glass trickling off him. He removed his jacket as he stepped through the shattered window and tossed it over to one of the two men. He cracked the knuckles on both of his hands as he towered over Ramone, who was acting as a human shield for Martha and Toya. He stared up at Shakur The God fearlessly with his fists at his sides.

"You wanna blindside the God, huh? Well, let's see what's shaking on some head-up sh—." Shakur The God was cut short by a swift three-punch combination by Ramone. He gave him two blows to the torso and then an uppercut, busting his mouth. Shakur The God staggered backwards and caught his equilibrium before he could hit the sidewalk. He turned back around, smiling sinisterly and showcasing his crimson teeth. He spat blood on the curb and wiped away the slimy blood strings hanging from his chin. Ramone rushed him, swinging on him again, but he proved to be far quicker than he thought, dodging him with super-fast reflexes.

Shakur The God ducked his attack and came back up, punching him in the jaw. Blood and spit flew from Ramone's mouth. He was clearly dazed, but he kept on swinging aimlessly at Shakur The God. Shakur The God smiled sinisterly again before firing on the young nigga's face three more times. Ramone plummeted towards the ground from the last punch, but before he could make contact with Shakur The God, he grabbed him by the front of his shirt. He held him up and looked into his eyes. His eyes were slits, and he was moaning while bleeding at the mouth. Shakur The God cocked back his fist and punched him as hard as he could. The force from the punch knocked Ramone free of his shirt and sent him tumbling down the sidewalk. He lay halfway off the curb in only his jeans and sneakers.

"Oh, hell no, don't nobody put their hands on my baby!" Martha shouted angrily at Shakur The God and pulled out a straight razor that the barber uses to shave his customers. A gleam swept up the length of it as she charged at Shakur The God swinging it wildly at him. Still holding Ramone's torn shirt in his hand, he moved swiftly, avoiding her attack. Unfortunately for him, she managed to slice his bare arm. He threw his head back, screaming in agony, dropping the torn shirt, and grabbing his bleeding wound. "You son of a bitch, I'ma carve yo ass up like a Thanksgiving turkey for putting your filthy fucking hands on my baby!"

Martha took several more swipes at Shakur The God. He avoided them all and kicked her in the stomach. Her eyes bucked, she dropped the straight razor and doubled over, holding her stomach. Shakur The God lifted up and came down with a strong backhand punch, leveling her with the ground. She lay there teetering between conscious and unconscious. Shakur The God harped up a slimy glob of mucus and spat it on her. The yellowish goo splattered against her cheek and slowly slid down.

"Aye, big man, I didn't hear no bell ring!" Ramone's voice rang from over Shakur The God's shoulder. When he turned around, he found the young nigga struggling to stand on wobbly legs with Toya holding his right arm.

"You got mad heart, shorty, but I'm done with playing witcho lil' ass," Shakur The God assured him. He turned to one of his homies, who lifted his shirt and took his gun out of his waistband. He cocked it, and when he went to turn around, a loud shot erupted, startling everyone. Shakur The God looked in the direction from where the shot came. He found Ramone bleeding at the mouth and holding himself up against the light post. Toya was standing in front of him protectively, scowling and holding Shakur The God's smoking revolver above her head. She brought the pistol down and leveled it at him. He could tell by her stance and grip on the piece this wasn't her first time handling one.

"That was a warning shot," Toya told him. She looked like a circus act with the left side of her face swollen from Shakur The

God assaulting her. "But this next one, I promise you, boo-boo, it's going right between your eyes if you don't drop that gun."

"This bitch has balls. I'll give her that," one of Shakur The God's goons said from beside him, drawing down on Toya. Shakur The God already had his gun pointed at her. "But tell us, shorty, what good is one measly ass piece against the two of ours?"

"I think mine will even the odds," Jabari said as he stepped forward with a black assault rifle. His car was parked at an angle in the middle of the street, and its trunk was wide open. "Allow me to introduce my girlfriend here, gentlemen. Her name is Sheila. Sheila is a Tavor-21 assault rifle manufactured by the lovely folks of Israel. She comes with a grenade launcher, night vision sight, and a silencer. Her standard magazine holds up to 30 rounds, but I increased its capacity so it can hold up to 100 rounds. In one minute, this gorgeous piece of foreign machinery can produce exactly 900 shots." Ramone whistled at the amount of bullets the assault rifle could disperse. "Now, you'll probably manage to hit a couple of us if you decide to squeeze those triggers. But I promise you, my right hand to God," he lifted his right hand, "one squeeze of mine will cut you all in half and guarantee you'll never get up again."

"Is that a fact?" the goon pointing his gun at them asked.

"You goddamn right it is," Jabari assured him with a scowl, placing his other hand on his deadly weapon. "But I'll tell you what, since you seem like a gambling man, let's leave it up to a game of chance." His nostrils flared, and he clenched his jaws, making them pulsate. He stared Shakur The God and his goons down as they did him. If it wasn't for the police sirens blaring as they headed to their location, there wouldn't be any noise at all.

"Aiight," Shakur The God broke the tension by throwing up his hand. "You've got this one, youngin', but rest assured, you and I are gonna settle this sometime in the near future," Shakur The God said to Ramone while passing his other goon the gun he'd taken from him. He slipped on his jacket and adjusted his collar before walking away. "Let's roll my Gs. Later, Jabari." The goons

lingered behind, mean mugging Jabari and them before tucking their bangaz and jogging up the block to catch up with Shakur The God.

Chapter 11

"It's all good, shorty. Let's get the hell out of here before Jake shows up," Jabari said to Toya placing his hand on her shoulder. She sighed with relief and lowered her gun. She helped Martha to her feet and asked if she was okay. She nodded and threw up some pinkish green slime with food particles in it.

"Yo Maduke's gon' be aiight?" Jabari asked Ramone while staring at her.

"She's dope sick," Ramone told him. He was watching his mother as well.

"You know I keep a lil' something, something on me in case of emergencies. I could bless you with it if you'd like."

"Good looking out on that and for tonight as well." Ramone shook up with him while holding his side with his other hand.

"Don't mention it, king. If the roles were reversed, I'm sure you'd come through in a clutch for ya boy," Jabari told him.

"No doubt. Yo, how you know homeboy?" Ramone asked Jabari as they headed back to his car.

"I did a lil' time with Blood on the island," Jabari replied. He hid his Tavor-21 inside of the secret compartment in the trunk of his car and slammed it shut.

Toya helped Martha into the backseat of Jabari's car and closed the door behind her.

"Yo, shorty, what was all that about back there?" Ramone asked.

"I was in the lil' Chinese takeout joint, ordering my usual when your mom came in trying to score from that asshole Shakur. He tried to dismiss her 'cause she already ran up a tab with him, but she wasn't trying to hear him. I guess she really needed her fix. Anyway, he got heated and started punching on her like she was a fucking man. I jumped in it trying to defend her, and, well, here we are now."

"That's good looking out. I appreciate you holding my mom's down in my absence and shit," Ramone said sincerely.

"Oh, it was nothing." Toya waved him off.

"Nah, ma, you put yourself in the crossfire for my OG, and you didn't have to. I owe you one for real, for real."

Toya nodded. "Aye, I'ma following you guys home, so I can help you with your moms. And before you say I don't have to, I want to, and I'm not taking no for an answer."

"Aiight," Ramone replied with a smirk and nod.

"Aye, lover boy, let's boogie before we end up in the bull-pen," Jabari hollered out the driver's window.

"We better get going," Toya said before taking off running to her car.

Ramone hopped into the front passenger seat of Jabari's car. He fired it up. Once Toya pulled up behind them, Jabari drove away, and she followed closely behind.

***

Jabari dropped Ramone and them off in Red Hook. He gave him a bag of dope for his mother's habit, shook up with him, and drove off. Ramone and Toya helped Martha up to his apartment on the twelfth floor. Ramone came up with every excuse in the book to try to get Toya not to come up to his apartment, but she insisted on helping him with his mother. The young nigga's stomach was doing summersaults thinking about what she was going to think when she saw his place. He had a little crush on her, and he didn't want to turn her off of him.

Fuck it, yo, either she gon' fuck with a nigga, or she isn't. It's whatever, Ramone thought as he held on to Martha with one hand and used his other to fish out his keys and open the apartment's door. Once he'd gotten it open, he pocketed the keys and gently kicked the door open. The door swung open, and everyone made their way inside. Toya looked around at everything inside of the apartment, and she definitely wasn't impressed. Her feelings towards Ramone didn't change either. In fact, she kind of expected his crib to look the way it did.

"Excuse my place," Ramone told Toya after catching her looking over his apartment.

The apartment had yellowing walls and brown water stains from the upstairs unit flooding. The only furniture inside of the living room was a raggedy black leather sofa. There was duct tape overlapping the cuts in the cushions and cotton hanging out the armrest of it. A thirty-inch box television set with a wire hanger used as an antenna sticking up out of it sat on top of a fifty-inch floor model television which didn't work. In addition to that, there were roaches crawling about. Toya made a disgusted face seeing a dark brown one scaling the kitchen counter with a white sack hanging from the back of it. She yelped when a gray rat scurried across her foot and made her jump back.

Ramone snickered and tried not to laugh, but he couldn't help it. "Hahahahahahahaha."

"Don't laugh, nigga. That shit not funny." Toya laughed and playfully punched his arm.

"Aye, you insisted on bringing your ass up here." Ramone grinned.

"That was just an excuse to spend more time witchu," Toya replied with a smile. She didn't mean to let it slip, but she decided to let it rock to see his reaction.

"Lemme find out." Ramone returned the smile. "Come on. Let's get her stripped down and into the shower."

"I don't wanna take a shower, baby. I need my medication," Martha told him with ballooning cheeks. She looked like she was about to throw up again.

"Your medication is right here, ma." He pulled it out of his pocket, holding it between his pinched fingers. She went to take it, but he snatched it away and pocketed it again. "You'll get it once you've showered and brushed your teeth."

Ramone and Toya helped Martha inside of the bathroom and sat her on the toilet. Toya twisted the dial for the showerhead and twisted the dials for the water. As the water sprayed, she tested its temperature and made sure it was to her liking.

"Look, I've never seen my old bird naked in my life, and I'm not trying to start now," Ramone told Toya in a hushed tone. "You

mind doing me a favor and washing her up while I gather her some underwear and pajamas to slip on?"

"Sure. No problem," Toya replied.

"Thanks, shorty." He patted her on the arm and headed out of the bathroom.

Once Ramone had left, Toya went about the task of helping Martha disrobe. She reeked of vomit, and she could smell a hint of shit on her. There were the classic signs of a fiend going through withdraws and needing a fix. Once Toya had gotten Martha stripped down to her dingy, lint ball pink bra and panties, she noticed something wrapped up in a discolored blue bandana. It was wedged in her cleavage.

"Ms. Martha, what is that?" Toya narrowed her eyes at it.

"My kit that I use to take my medication," Martha told her as she pulled out the bandana and sat it on the kitchen sink. "I feel like I'ma throw-up again." She spun around, lifted the toilet's lid, and got down on her knees. She hurled inside of the bowl as the bathroom began to fog from the hot shower water. While she was puking, Toya snuck a peek at what was inside the bandana. She found a syringe, a 20-inch beige tourniquet, a marred spoon, a small tube of water, and a couple of cotton balls. She rolled the items back up in the bandana and set it aside.

Martha farted while she was down on her knees. She looked to Toya with ropes of slimy saliva hanging from her chin. "Excuse me, baby, but I'm sick as a dog. I gotta poop, so if you don't mind." She gestured towards the door with her head, suggesting she leave. "I'm sure I can manage to shower myself."

"Okay." Toya nodded. She touched Martha's shoulder affectionately as she headed for the door. Ramone appeared in the doorway cradling underwear and pajamas with the bag of dope on them. He passed everything to Toya. "She wants her privacy, so I'ma let her shower and get dressed," she told him as she lay what he'd given her on top of the bathroom sink. As soon as she did, a black roach scurried away, but she acted like she didn't see it for fear of embarrassing Ramone further.

"Aiight. That's cool," Ramone replied as he stood outside the door with his arms folded across his chest. Toya came out of the bathroom, pulling the door shut behind her.

Ghost & Tranay Adams

Chapter 12

Toya examined Ramone's body like a doctor would, checking him out thoroughly. He was lean and had six-pack abs. The old gunshot wounds and keloid scars were a testament to his survival in the concrete jungle. Ramone's marred body, coupled with his rough and rugged demeanor, turned her on.

Toya held Ramone by his chin and took a good look at his injuries. He had a few small blood cuts, bruises, and some swelling to the side of his face.

"I've gotta clean you up. You wouldn't by any chance have a first aid kit, would you?" Toya asked him.

"Yeah, there's one inside the kitchen cabinet above the stove." Ramone directed with his finger.

"Okay, I'll be right back." Toya went inside the kitchen. As soon as she opened the cabinets above the stove, she was startled by the presence of a big ass rat. She shouted and jumped back, placing her hands over her breasts. Her heart nearly leaped out of her chest.

Ramone ran inside of the kitchen, ready to throw hands, thinking someone had broken in his crib. He relaxed when he saw that it was a rodent that had frightened Toya. He smacked the vermin aside and took down the yellow first aid kit with a red cross on it. He passed it to Toya. She took it and then by his hand, journeying inside of the bedroom. The only thing inside of the bedroom was a mattress on the floor, a fan in the corner, and a scarred wooden dresser with some of the faces of the drawers missing. The room was tidy, but there were roaches here and there. Toya jumped upon the mattress screaming when a rodent ran across her foot. She sighed with relief when she saw the filthy rat squeezed inside of a hole in the wall on the other side of the bedroom.

Ramone couldn't help feeling embarrassed and ashamed of his apartment. Although he loved having Toya around to keep him company, he wanted her to go home so he could stop being so uptight. He'd never tell her that for fear of offending her and causing her to run off.

"You mind if we, uh, sat Indian style on your mattress while I do this?" Toya asked, still standing up in the bed. Ramone nodded, took her hand, and helped her down upon the bed. She sat Indian-style and popped the locks of the yellow first aid kit. She removed the items she'd need to tend to Ramone's injuries and sat the kit aside. Ramone hopped up on the bed and sat down Indian-style across from her.

Toya dabbed a cloth with a bottle of green alcohol and used it to clean the small cuts on his face. He winced in pain, so she stopped, but he insisted she kept going. Ramone studied her face as she tended his wounds. She was hands down the most beautiful young lady he'd laid eyes on, and that was saying a lot, especially for her not to have any makeup on. Toya blushed and smiled like she'd been told to say cheese for a picture.

"What? Why are you looking at me like that?" Toya asked as she continued to clean his cuts.

"Shorty, if I told you, you'd think I was running game, so let's change the subject," Ramone told her.

"Aiight," Toya replied continuing with her task. Suddenly, she stopped tending to his face and sat up on the bed. "Okay, this shit is gonna drive me up the wall, so I gotta know."

Ramone frowned with concern. "What's up, ma?"

"I gotta know what you were thinking when I caught you staring at me."

"It's really that big of a deal?"

"Yes. I've gotta know."

"Okay, well, I was thinking about how beautiful you are."

He confessed. She blushed and smiled harder, dropping her head. She could literally feel the butterflies flying around in her stomach.

Girl, you really let this young-ass project nigga run game on you? Don't let that beautiful shit fool you. He's more than likely like the rest, niggaz learning the game younger and younger these days.

Ramone tilted her chin up, so she'd be looking in his eyes. "On gang, this real shit I'm hitting you with. Look at my face,

look in my eyes." Toya did exactly like he'd told her. His eyes held the truth, and his face was stern and convincing. If he was lying to her, then he was a damn good actor and deserved at the very least an Oscar nomination. "Now, tell me I'm lying."

"I believe you." Toya packed everything back inside of the First Aid kit, locked it, and rose from the bed with it cradled in her arms. She was on her way out the door when she suddenly stopped in her tracks and walked back over to Ramone. She pecked him on his cheek. "Thank you."

"For what exactly?"

"For being so sweet."

"Only spitting facts."

"I'm sure." Toya blushed and made her way out of the bedroom.

Ramone thought about his mother. She'd been in the bathroom for a while and hadn't come out yet. Deciding to check on her, he rapped on the bathroom door and called her name. He didn't receive a response, so he opened the door and became overwhelmed by a hot fog from the shower water. The bathroom was humid. The walls were sweating, and so was the medicine cabinet mirror. When the fog emerged from the bathroom and into the hallway, Ramone was presented with his mother. Martha was slumped on the toilet dressed in her bra and panties. She was in a dope head nod. Her legs were outstretched in front of her, and both her arms were hanging at her sides. A beige tourniquet was tied around her left arm, and the syringe she'd used to shoot the dope with was hanging out of her vein.

Ramone removed the syringe out of his mother's arm, capped, and trashed it. He removed the tourniquet from around her arm and sat it on the sink. He stood upright, took a breath, and looked down at his mother with pity. She'd never really been a good mother, but she was all he and Jayshawn had since their old man split. Growing up, when he would see the loving relationships between other kids and their mothers, it would make him envy them. He found himself hating his mother and his father for not giving him and his brother the family every child deserved and

desired. His emotions had him terribly confused. He found himself hating the ground his mother walked on one minute and loving her beyond measure the next.

Ramone kneeled down to his mother with his hands dangling between his knees.

"Despite the way I act sometimes, I love you, ma. I really, really do." Ramone confessed. "I just want you to get off this dope for good and do right by bruh and I. Pops is gone, so you're all we have left besides each other. It would be dope to have all of us together as a family for once. Celebrating Thanksgiving, Christmas, Labor Day, and all the other holidays together. Breaking out the grill and barbequing on Fridays like Pops used to." He grinned, thinking about the good times and those that could manifest in the future.

"I've gotta plan, momma. I've gotta plan to get you clean and acting like a mother. A real mother, like those me and bro used to watch on TV. You'll see, everything is going to be aiight. I promise you, ma." He grasped her hand and rubbed the top of her hand with his thumb. He stood up and kissed his mother on her forehead. He hadn't the slightest inkling that Toya had been watching him from the doorway the entire time.

"Knock, knock," Toya said, turning into the doorway. She saw Ramone attempting to pick up his mother. "You need some help?"

"Nah, I think I've got it. I've been hitting the gym lately." He smirked. "Check out the gun show," He flexed his biceps like a tanned bodybuilder on stage during a competition. She laughed and placed her hand over her mouth.

Ramone scooped his mother in his arms and carried her inside her bedroom. He laid her across the bed and left Toya watching her. Toya swept Martha's hair aside and studied her face. She hadn't noticed it before, but even as a dope fiend, she was remarkably beautiful. She figured she had men chasing her back in the day when she was in her prime. It really tripped her out how a person can be up one minute and down the next. Life was truly like a seesaw.

King of the Trenches

Ramone returned to the bedroom with an old, dented toolbox and a silver chain with a shackle attached to the end of it. He sat the items on the side of the bed and then attached the silver link chain to the wall, using a drill and bolts. Holding the chain in both of his hands, he pulled it and yanked it hard. The chain proved to be secure and durable.

"Are you sure about this, Ramone? I mean, jailing your mother and all?" Toya asked while holding Martha's hand affectionately. "Don't you think it would be better to just get her checked into rehab?"

"Hahahahahaha. Yo, you really don't know my moms, shorty. She'd wind up escaping one of them joints like them white niggaz in Alcatraz. Trust me. This is the best and only way."

Toya looked at Martha and took a deep breath. "Okay. You are her son, so you know what's best for her."

"No doubt."

Ramone made sure the chain could reach as far as the bathroom and the bed before he locked the shackle around his mother's wrist. He left the bedroom and returned with a cardboard box. Using thumbtacks, he hung up old pictures of them as a family to give her motivation to get clean. He nailed a banner over the door that read: You can do it. We believe in you. We love you, mom.

Ramone took a can of red spray paint out of the cardboard box. He shook it up and spray-painted motivational quotes on all the walls inside of the bedroom. He even put some on the ceiling. Once he was done, he tossed the can of spray inside of the box and smacked imaginary dirt off his hands.

He caressed his mother's cheek with the back of his hand and then kissed her on the cheek. Toya spread a sheet over her and kissed her on the side of her forehead.

Chapter 13

"Come on," Ramone told Toya as he lifted up the cardboard box. He threw his head towards the door and walked through it. Toya followed behind him, pulling the door shut on her way out. Ramone pulled out a key and locked the door to his mother's bedroom. He had the only key to the bedroom, and he planned to keep it that way. He was going to see to it that his mother finally got off dope. After he stashed the cardboard box underneath the kitchen sink, Ramone took a glass down from the kitchen cupboard and washed it out. He filled the glass halfway, turned off the faucet, and leaned back against the counter. He took a long drink of water and wiped his mouth.

"Ramone, I don't know if you know it, but chances are your mom is going to get pretty nasty while going through this detox," Toya told him, leaning up against the counter and placing her hand on top of his. He glanced at her hand on top of his, liking the feeling of her coming so close. "My Aunt Grace performed like a demon when we locked her up to kick her habit."

"I hear you, lil' baby, and I'm not sweating it. I'ma soldier up and make sure my old bird gets through this shit."

Toya smirked and rubbed the side of his face. "You love her, don't you? I mean, that day at the hospital, you were as cold as a block of ice toward her, but at the end of the day, you truly love her, you and your brother." Ramone nodded.

"You should find comfort in knowing that she loves you too. You see how she came at ol' dude you were squabbling with? Momma drew that blade and was about ready to chop his big ass into rows sushi." She mimicked Martha, trying to poke Shakur The God, full of holes with her knife. She and Ramone laughed.

"Yeah, Maduke's something else. From what I hear, she was a real firecracker back in the day. She used to carry a pair of nunchucks and a straight razor wherever she went. Big bruh said she'd bring it to whomever. It didn't matter how big or small they were."

"I bet. Do you mind? I'm a lil' thirsty." Toya smirked, pointing at his glass of water.

"Oh, sure," Ramone replied, passing her the glass. He watched as she drank what was left of the water and sat the glass in the sink. She turned around and held eye contact with him. They both had jovial expressions on their faces, searching for the right thing to say next. "Soooo, uh, look, it's getting late. I could walk you down to yo car if you'd like."

She tilted her head to the side and looked at him strangely. "Damn, it's like that? You just gon' kick me to the curb now?"

"Nah, I'm just saying. It's getting mad late, and I figure you may want to be getting home."

"Maybe I don't wanna go home. Maybe I'd like to spend the night with you," she said in a seductive voice, allowing her finger to slide down over both his lips.

"You really wanna kick it here with all these roaches and rats running through here? I know where you laying yo head couldn't be that bad, shorty."

A great sadness came over Toya. Her eyes watered, and she lowered her head. "If you only knew, Ramone. If you only knew." She looked back up at him wiping her tears away with her thumbs.

He felt for her. Seeing someone so sweet, kind, and beautiful as her in despair was fucking with him. He wanted to do nothing more than protect her like the delicate flower she was and ensure her safety.

"What's wrong, Toya? Tell me, what's the matter?" Ramone asked, holding her at arm's length. Toya tried to tell him what the cause of her sudden breakdown was, but he couldn't understand her. She was sobbing and trying to talk at the same time. "Come here, ma." She walked into his arms, and he held her tight. He rubbed her back and kissed the top of her head. "Shhhhh. It's going to be aiight. I got you. I promise."

Toya stopped crying and pulled herself together. She looked up at Ramone with a tear-streaked face. "Is it...is it okay if I stay here with you tonight?"

"Sure. Not a problem. You can crash here for as long as you want," he told her. "I just gotta run it by my roommates, but I'm sure they won't mind."

"Roommates?" her forehead wrinkled.

"Yeah. These roaches and rats." He smirked.

"You're so silly." She smiled and playfully hit him. She then laid her head against his chest and held onto him. "You know what's kray?"

"Speak on it."

"Right here right now, in the heart of one of the most dangerous housing complexes in the city, I feel the safest I have ever been in your arms."

"Word? I gotta write that down. That's a good one." Ramone grinned.

"Whatever, boy, come on. Let's go lay down." Toya smiled and led him to his bedroom.

***

Ramone gave Toya an old fading Fubu T-shirt of his to wear to bed. He lay back in bed with his fingers interlocked behind his head. He was wearing an old dingy T-shirt that was torn at the collar and basketball shorts. He focused his attention on the door when he heard Toya return to the bedroom. She closed the door behind her and turned around to him. She spread open her arms and turned around in a circle.

"So, how do I look?" Toya asked.

"As always, you look beautiful," Ramone replied with a smirk.

"Thank you." She grinned as she crawled in bed beside him. He scooted further to the opposite side of the bed and gave her one of his pillows.

Toya got comfortable in bed and pulled the blanket over her. She lay on her side with one hand underneath the side of her face. She stared at the wall while Ramone stared up at the ceiling. Besides the crickets chirping and the residents chopping it up on the ground floor, the bedroom was exceptionally quiet.

"Ramone, do you mind holding me like you did earlier in the kitchen?" Toya asked him. "It's the only way I think I can fall asleep. I just need to feel safe, ya know? Protected."

"Yeah. I can hold you." Ramone turned on his side and wrapped his arm around Toya. She scooted back against him, interlocked her fingers with his, and pulled him tighter around her. Relieved, she took a breath, and a smile curled her lips. "What's that I feel against my ass?" she looked at him from the corners of his eyes.

"Oh, shit, my bad, shorty. I didn't mean to—"

"You're good. I understand. You're a young man with raging hormones, and you've gotta attractive young lady in your bed. If I were you, I'd be excited too."

"That's why I fucks with you, ma. You mad cool." He shut his eyes and fixed himself in bed.

"Ramone?"

"What's the deal?"

"I'm ready to tell you why I broke down in the kitchen now."

"It's all good, lil' baby, don't worry about it."

"Nah. I really want you to know. Besides, I've never told anyone, and I need to vent."

Ramone opened his eyes. "Aiight. Go ahead, tell me."

Toya's story both saddened and sickened Ramone. When she was just twelve years old, her mother met an Arabian billionaire oil tycoon that swept her off her feet and promised her a life fit for a princess. Although the tycoon was happy to take her as his wife, he refused to play stepdaddy to another nigga's kids. One day, Toya and her father awoke to find her mother gone along with most of her belongings. Toya and her old man were devastated and heartbroken.

With Toya's mother out of the picture, in order to make ends meet, her old man sold crack on the side to support them, in addition to being a security guard. Eventually, the money from selling drugs had gotten so good, he quit his 9-5 and started hustling full-time. In the beginning, it was only him and Toya, so they divided up the work between them until they could put

reliable niggaz on. Toya was tasked with cooking the product, chopping it, weighing it, and preparing it for distribution. Sometimes she had to play the role of the mule, transporting the merchandise to and from specified locations. Her old man, on the other hand, handled the distribution aspect of the business. Once things took off, he brought on cooks, trap boys, and some local hittas in case drama arose.

Although Toya's mother had bounced on them, things began to settle and return to how they once were—or so Toya thought. Her Pops had started getting high on his own supply. She didn't know what it was about crack, but it made him horny, extremely horny. First, he was fucking with the hoodrats that naturally came along with being a ghetto celebrity. Then he started tricking off with barely legal prostitutes. When he'd grown tired of them, he started in on her. The night she'd lost her virginity to him, she'd tried desperately to fight him off, but it wasn't to any avail. He was a grown man and far stronger than her.

After the first time, the sexual assaults occurred frequently, and though she didn't like it, she'd sort of got used to it. Her Pops convinced her that them having sex was a spiritual healing for both of them. It was the only way they could get over the emotional scars her mother abandoning them caused. Toya deemed the relationship between her and her father repulsive. When she tried to appeal to the humanity in him to convince him to stop their incestuous involvement, he put a gun to her head and threatened to kill her if she ever tried to leave him. From then on, Toya was scared straight! She didn't dare to leave her father. She tried to gas herself up to kill him, but she couldn't bring herself to do it because he was her father, and somewhere deep down inside of her, she still loved him.

"Shhhhh. Shhhhhh," Ramone shushed Toya as he held her in his arms. He kissed the back of her head and tightened his hold on her. He felt the vibration of her body and shuddering of her head as she cried and sniffled. "Relax, shorty, I got you now. And I promise you, my right hand to God, no one is ever gonna hurt you again. I'ma take care of your old man. That's my word."

"Can you—can you do me a favor, please?" Toya asked, wiping her snotty nose with the sleeve of her shirt.

"Anything, ma, just tell me, and it's done."

"I know we haven't known each other long, so you don't have to mean it. But I just—I just really need to hear you say you love me right now. Can you tell me that, please? I promise I won't hold—"

"I love you, ShaToya," Ramone cut her short.

The moment he told her, she broke down sobbing and trembling.

"Again, please."

"I love you. I love you. And I'll always love you, ShaToya Miller."

Toya cried in his arms until she eventually fell aside with dry tears on her face and crusty snot below her nose. Ramone confirmed her sleeping by her softly snoring. He had to piss so bad that his balls were aching, and it felt like his dick was going to explode. Carefully, he eased his arm from around her, slid out of bed, and snuck out of the bedroom. He used the bathroom, washed his hands, and was surprised when he returned to his bedroom.

Toya stood before him in all of her heavenly glory. Her chocolate body was curvy and without any flaws worth mentioning. Her C-cup breasts sat up perfectly on her chest, her stomach was flat, and her buttocks were pillow-soft. Her hair lay sprawled over her shoulders and over her face, obscuring her vision of him. Ramone took her in from head to toe, thinking how much she looked like a goddess. He licked his top row of teeth and rubbed his hands together in anticipation of the blessing she was about to bestow upon him.

Toya walked her way over to Ramone and wrapped her arms around his neck. Kissing him gently, she slipped him a little tongue and closed her eyes. They made out slow and sensually with murmurs of pleasure escaping between their lips. Ramone, with his eyes closed, rubbed his hands up and down her back. Then up and down her globes. They were big, round, and warm.

Toya nibbled on his earlobe and caused a tingling sensation to travel down his back. He gasped, with his eyes closed and his mouth hanging open. She softly bit down his neck and then licked up it. He continued to rub his hands up and down her back while basking in the state of euphoria she'd put him in. She'd begun sucking on his neck when she felt his piece nudging against her.

"Yo, shorty, I'm feeling you, and I want this, but I gotta ask. What brought this on all of a sudden?"

"You're gonna take care of that monster I call father, so it's only right that I give you something in return."

Upon hearing this, Ramone's eyes popped open, and he held her at arm's length. "Look, you don't have to let me smash 'cause I told you I was gon' take care of ya old man. I'm doing that on the strength you were trying to protect my moms. You came to the hospital to make sure I was aiight and shit, you just straight up good people. I fucks with you hard body."

"Well, I could pay you if you'd like. Lemme get my purse." Toya turned to grab her purse, and he grabbed her arm, stopping her in her tracks.

"Nah, you don't understand. I don't wanna be compensated for handling that piece of shit." Ramone assured her. "All I want is for you to be loyal to me and to have my back like I'ma always have yours. Nothing more, nothing less."

Toya nodded understandingly and cupped his face. She kissed him affectionately all over his face and then one last time on the lips. Still holding his face, she looked into his eyes with a smirk. "You're making it difficult not to fall in love with you, Ramone. I've never had a boyfriend, but if I did, I'd want him to be exactly like you. There's absolutely nothing I would change about you."

Grinning, Ramone picked up her panties, bra, and the shirt he'd given her to sleep in. He helped her slip everything on and led her over to his bed. She closed her eyes and laid the side of her face against his chest while he held her. Listening to Toya's soft snoring put Ramone to sleep. Her listening to the rhythm and drum-like pattern of his heart eventually put her to sleep as well.

Chapter 14

Cruzito's was a bar located in the Heart of Harlem between Adam Clayton Powell Boulevard and 125th Street. Lowlifes and unsavory characters alike were permanent fixtures in the seedy establishment. And they were just as welcome as anyone else looking to drop in to shoot the breeze over a couple of cold ones. Interestingly enough, for Cruzito's to be a hole in the wall known to be the epicenter for those who chose to live their lives on the wrong side of the law, the violence there was kept to a minimum. This was largely due to the owner being connected to some very powerful players in the underworld.

Tonight, Cruzito's would be used to hold a meeting that his niece Olivia had arranged. She had gotten her uncle to let her use his place for what she dubbed her 'Meeting of the minds'. He wasn't with the idea of closing down early, but a few dollars got him to change his mind and grant Olivia a full run of the place. Olivia sent an invite to the fiancés, girlfriends, and wives of some of the most successful kingpins of the five boroughs. She knew they wouldn't come out on an invitation alone, so she added a $2,000 dollar incentive. She figured that was enough bread to make the women at least curious to find out what she wanted.

By the time the clock struck nine, luxury vehicle after luxury vehicle drove up and parked in front of Cruzitos. It looked like a car club had assembled out in front of the bar. Every last one of the whips was waxed so fine any onlookers could see their reflection in it. The grand total price of the cars came out to a little over 2 million dollars. Well, at least that was what Blanca had estimated as she stood out front. Shorty was a slim joint, two shades darker than her cousin Olivia. She had two handfuls of breasts and a small bubble butt. Although she was a female, she wasn't any less dangerous than the men wandering the Brooklyn streets she affectionately called home.

Her long, curly black hair was pulled back in a bun, and her lips were painted with a clear coat of lip gloss. Blanca was wearing a black bowtie and a white button-down shirt underneath

a black vest. She held a retractable taser at her side that doubled as a baton. Its sole purpose was to neutralize any threat the ladies may pose. Though she doubted she and Olivia would have any problems. She reasoned it was always better to be safe than sorry.

Blanca watched as the invited guests stepped out of their vehicles one by one. They were all dolled up and looked like they hopped off the covers of the most recent VOGUE magazines. Toya didn't know any of them personally, but she was familiar with them in passing. She was well-versed in the men they had an association with.

The first woman to step out onto the scene had driven there in a maroon Ferrari Purosangue truck with smoke-black tinted windows. She was a cinnamon brown honey who wore her short hair like Halle Berry in the 90s. She was wearing a wide brim straw hat and a white halter top underneath blue denim overalls that looked like they were painted on her voluptuous body.

Lucinda walked upon the curb rummaging through her big designer bag until she found what she was looking for: the envelope containing the golden invitation to the meeting that came along with the $2,000 dollars. She made her way over to the entrance of Cruzito's, where Blanca directed her to stand on the line.

The second whip was definitely one that screamed boss status. It was a platinum-grey Rolls-Royce Ghost with limousine tinted windows and original chrome rims and tires. The driver's door popped open, and a muscular white man in his mid-to-late forties stepped out. He sported a baldhead and a five o'clock shadow with sprinkles of gray in it. He worked as a chauffeur and a bodyguard as well. Not only could he handle virtually any firearm one could name, but he was skilled in Krav Maga, which is the world's most effective and dangerous form of hand-to-hand combat.

The chauffeur scanned the area for any threats to the security of the woman he had sworn to protect. Seeing the surroundings didn't show any immediate threat, he opened the backdoor for his charge and helped her out. She was a five-foot-five number, about twenty-three years old, slender in build, and as cute as can be. She

was light-skinned with a freckled face and flat-ironed auburn hair that fell down to her back. Her attire was a two-piece black jean outfit and loosely laced butter Timbs. Shorty's name was Piffany, but she went by the name Bubbles. As the chauffeur shut the backdoor behind her, she withdrew the envelope containing her gold invitation from her bag and made her way over to the entrance of the bar.

The third vehicle was one of luxury and sophistication. It was a midnight blue Jaguar XJR with leather peanut butter interior. Trinicia swung open the driver's door and stepped out onto the pavement, one stiletto high heel shoe at a time. She grabbed her handbag and fixed her fluffy quarter-length mink on her frame. She slammed the driver's door, swung her long, bouncy, curly hair from side to side, and slipped on her designer shades. Pulling her gold invitation from the recess of her mink, her chocolate bougie ass walked towards the entrance of the bar with the cockiness of a superstar runway model.

The fourth and final car was a white BMW X6 with blood-red interior. It had red-tinted windows and factory alloy rims. Its driver was an Amazonian with a big bust and an even bigger rump. This pretty, chubby face woman went by Echo. She was undeniably quiet and timid. She moved with the air of someone who had the burden of carrying a world full of hurt on her shoulders. The first thing Blanca noticed about her was she was wearing shades at night. The second thing she noticed was she seemed afraid and paranoid. She was looking around like she expected someone to jump out of the shadows and ravage her at any moment.

The four women stood in line outside of Cruzito's bar, where they were greeted and patted down thoroughly by Blanca. Once she had finished performing the task, she directed them towards the back storage room where Olivia was waiting for them. One by one, the ladies fell in step behind each other and made their way towards the storage room. Blanca scanned the block before turning the sign hanging on the door from OPEN to CLOSED. She vanished inside of the bar and slammed the door shut behind her.

***

Olivia wore a smirk on her lips as she watched her guests enter the backroom. She was wearing a tan, form-fitting Vera Wang dress and clutching a handbag. Her hair was styled in a Bob with a Chinese bang hanging right above her eyes. The diamonds in her ears twinkled, and so did the diamond tennis bracelet decorating her neck. Normally for something like this, she'd had worn something more casual, but it was important to her that these ladies knew that she came from money just like them. She figured they would be more prone to listening to her that way.

Olivia greeted her guests and motioned for them to sit down at the conference table at the center of the room. The women fixed the chairs to their comfort and waited for what was to come next. Blanca came through the backroom door and closed it behind her. She made her way around the table, taking in all of the faces of those in attendance. She wasn't trying to intimidate them but let them all see the gun holstered at her side. This way, if any of them thought about trying anything and the taser she had wasn't enough, then maybe the fact she was packing would make them reconsider.

Blanca posted up in one of the four corners of the room and folded her arms across her chest. She kept a close eye on everyone sitting at the table as Olivia sat her handbag on the table and addressed her guests.

"By a show of hands, how many of you ladies would love to become millionaires almost overnight?" Olivia asked. She looked around the table, and all of the ladies' hands were raised. "Good. I'd like to introduce you all to the narcotic that's gonna do that." She plucked a small baggie out of her cleavage and tossed it onto the table in front of Lucinda. Lucinda picked up the baggie and took a peek inside of it.

"Girl, this supposed to be the drug that's gon' make us millionaires almost overnight? This ain't nothing but some heroine." Lucinda said like it wasn't a big deal. She was expecting this new

drug of Olivia's to knock her socks off, but she winded up being disappointed when she found out what it was.

"Aye, lemme see that, boo," Bubbles told Lucinda. She received the baggie from her a moment later.

"Lemme see it once you finish, mamas." Trinicia watched as Bubbles examined the contents of the baggie.

"Okay," Bubbles replied.

"So lemme get this straight, sis, you dropped two racks on us each, just for us to come way up here for you to show us your dope? I can't front. I thought you was gon' hip us to some new designer shit that hit the scene, but this is just regular ol' Boy. You can get that anywhere, Uptown or Downtown." Lucinda told Olivia and sat back in her seat. Trinicia was sitting beside her, sniffing the contents of the baggie.

"Nah, I think shorty wants us to turn our hubbies on to her product," Bubbles tried to guess the angle Olivia was coming from. "Look, if this was some move for you to try to persuade us to get our dudes to cop their drugs from you, lemme tell you, Trayveon is one fish that's not gon' bite this bait, he gets his shit cheap as fuck. I doubt you can beat his current plug's prices or the quality of his dope. He can step on his work three times, and it will still be 70 percent pure."

"I hear all of your gripes, but lemme assure you, ladies, this isn't your ordinary dope," Olivia said as she paced the floor with her hands behind her back. "It's called The Rebirth. It's genetically engineered to be ten times more addictive than regular heroin. In fact, it's been proven that once you get hooked on The Rebirth, there's no way you can get off it."

All of the women exchanged intrigued glances hearing this. "A dope fiend will slit his own mother's throat to get his hands on it. The Rebirth has already hit the East Coast. The Dominicans are already pushing it, slanging it hand over fist, and they're making a fucking killing. This shit is the new wave, and I don't know about y'all, but I'm getting in on it." Her eyes took in the women as they spoke among each other, nodding their heads to what she was saying.

A smirk formed at the corner of her mouth, seeing she was gaining favor with them. She decided to press them further. "I'm telling y'all, with this Rebirth, we can take over the game. We could sew up all five boroughs with this shit. I'm talking Brooklyn, the Bronx, Queens, Manhattan, and Staten Island."

Chapter 15

"Sis, I feel what you're saying, but I think most of our men are not going to want to roll with this." Bubbles stated. The rest of the women nodded in agreement with what she was saying. Some of the men had been warring with the neighboring boroughs on and off for years over one thing or another. There were too many casualties for them to look the other way and do business together.

"She's right," Lucinda added her two cents. "I don't see Jock's vindictive ass making peace with Hog after what they've been through."

"You're right, mamas, I've been fucking with Hog since my freshmen year of high school, and I've never known my man to let go of a grudge," Bubbles admitted.

"Y'all keep talking about the men, fuck them niggaz! I'm not trying to have the men in on this thing of ours no way." Olivia stated, drawing confused looks from the rest of the ladies.

"What are you saying?" Trinicia asked.

"That's what I want to know," Lucinda spoke up.

"I'm saying we form a coalition of boss ass bitches, with all of us sitting here at this table," Olivia told her. "Now, my connect is willing to give us a fifteen percent discount on the weight as long as we agree to buy from him and only him. I figure we start off with three mill in product. Between the five of us, that shouldn't be hard to come up with." She looked around at the women nodding reassuringly and whispering among each other. Seeing a hand raised at the corner of her eye, she looked and saw Trinicia with her hand up. She pointed at her.

"Okay, so what about Jake? Once we get shit popping, they're going to be on us like flies on shit," Trinicia said.

"Twelve gets what? Fifty, sixty geez a year?" Olivia asked rhetorically. "That bag is not big enough to take care of a family, especially not in high ass New York. We'll hit their hand to look the other way while we do our thang. I figure as long as we keep the bodies to a minimum, we'll be aiight." The women nodded in agreement.

"Ok, there's still the issue with the men. What do you propose we do about them?" Trinicia asked.

Olivia looked in the women's eyes that rounded out the table. Her eyes were stern and piercing. "I'll give you ladies one wild guess."

The women knew exactly what Olivia was getting at then. She wanted them to kill their significant others so that they could sit at the head of their empires. The women exchanged glances with each other, thinking about the proposal Olivia had placed on the table. Although all their guys had taken great care of them financially, they didn't like the fact that they had mistresses, talked down to them, and used their money to control them. For these reasons, the women liked the idea of bossing up and governing their own organization.

"You mind giving us a minute to talk amongst ourselves privately?" Lucinda asked Olivia.

"Sure thing," Olivia grabbed her handbag and walked out of the room. One of the girls shut and locked the door behind her. She posted up outside the door with her arms folded across her chest, tapping her foot impatiently, wondering what was going to be the girls' decision. She felt like she needed a little something to calm her nerves, so she fished inside of her handbag for a thin silver case. She popped it open and revealed a row of perfectly rolled joints. She placed one between her lips and pulled out a lighter.

Olivia found herself having trouble trying to ignite a flame with her lighter. She shook it up and tried again, but it still didn't work. Seeing her growing frustration, Blanca sat the bucket of ice containing the golden bottle of Ace of Spades and the four champagne flutes down on the pool table.

"Lemme get that for you," Blanca said as she pulled out a Zippo lighter. She flipped it open with the flick of her wrist and produced a blue flame. Cupping her hand around Olivia's joint with one hand, she brought the lighter around with the other. Its blue flame licked at the tip of the joint until a cherry was born.

"Thank you," Olivia told her. She sucked on the end of the joint and then blew out a cloud of smoke. Blanca saw the anxiousness written over her face and the way she was tapping her foot. Right off, she knew she was growing annoyed with whatever was weighing heavily on her mind.

"What's the deal?" Blanca asked her as she closed the top of her lighter and pocketed it. Olivia gave her the rundown of what she'd discussed with the girls and how she was now waiting for their verdict. "Well, if them hoes know what's good for them, then they'll get with our program. If not, we'll roll with Plan B."

Olivia zeroed in on the bottle of Ace of Spades wedged inside the bucket of ice cubes sitting on the pool table. If her guests refused to go along with her master plan, she couldn't afford for them to go running back to their significant others and blabbing about what they discussed there that night. So, she had Blanca taint the bubbly contained inside of the champagne bottle with cyanide.

Olivia replayed what she'd rehearsed in front of the full-body mirror inside of her bedroom before she left for that night's meeting. She had just finished stepping into her Victoria's Secret panties and slipping on her bra when she had gotten into character.

"No?" Olivia asked, looking disappointed with their girls' decision. She bowed her head, took a defeated breath, and then looked back up at her reflection. "I really hate to hear that. I was looking forward to our union. Well, thanks for at least entertaining my offer. Say, just so ladies know it's no hard feelings, how about you have a drink with me before you leave?" she presented her most charming smile. "That's it. I got it. I fucking got it in the bag. I should have been a pinche actress on Broadway," she said excitedly before dipping off to the other side of the bedroom to get dressed for that night.

"I really hope it doesn't lead to Plan B, but if they pull out of this deal, mamita, then we've gotta do what we've gotta do. You feel me?" Olivia asked Blanca. She gave her a knowing glance which answered her question and dapped her up. The sound of the

door being unlocked drew Olivia and Blanca's attention. They turned around, and Lucinda stuck her head out of the door.

"Can I have a word with you?" Lucinda asked with a dead-serious expression.

"Sure," Olivia replied.

She listened closely as Lucinda whispered into her ear. "I get it. She has kids with him, so I don't blame her," Lucinda whispered to her some more, and her face balled up angrily.

"If it's like that, she shouldn't have a problem with handling him. Yo, lemme holla at lil' mama, tell her to come out here."

Lucinda stuck her head back inside of the room and called Echo over to the door. Echo stepped out of the door with her head bow fidgeting her fingers. She was a five-foot-nine BBW with a complexion so pale she could almost pass for a white woman. She was a pear-shaped woman who wore a Cleopatra-styled wig and oversized designer shades. She was dripping in designer, Gucci down to the socks, with the handbag to match.

The woman hadn't made as much as a peep during the entire meeting. Every now and then, Olivia would glance in her direction. Her quiet demeanor and the fact that she was wearing shades at night made Olivia suspicious of her. So, she wasn't surprised that out of the ladies who had an issue with going along with the plan, it was her.

Lucinda closed the door behind her and stood alongside Echo. She rubbed her back comfortingly and told her to tell Olivia what she told her.

"Look, Devonte ain't worth shit, but I love him. I love him with all that I am. We have three beautiful kids together, and we plan to get married," Echo told Olivia, her voice cracking emotionally.

"I know you may think I'm a fool for still being with him after what he's done to me, but I can't bring myself to kill him. I—I just can't—maybe—maybe someone else could do it for me. If—If I— I did it, then I know I wouldn't be able to live with myself." She sniffled as a tear slid down from her left eye. She took a few Kleenexes from her handbag and dabbed it away.

Her cellphone rang, and she pulled it from her back pocket. Instantly, she started trembling with fear and sobbing. Her reaction drew concerned expressions from the women present. They were wondering what was going on. "It's—it's him. It's Devonte. He wants to know where I am. I've been gone too long. I've gotta hurry up and get back." Echo went running out of the bar, but Lucinda grabbed her by her arm. She pulled her back beside her.

"Girl, no, you're not going back to that nigga. Are you crazy? That mothafucka is a monster!" Lucinda told her.

"Monster?" Olivia asked.

"Show her, Echo! Show her what that fucking animal did to you," Lucinda demanded.

Echo's cellphone stopped ringing, and then it started right back up again. She sobbed louder and louder, jumping up and down. She was clearly terrified of her baby daddy. "Oh, my God, what am I going to do? I told him I was going grocery shopping. If I show up home without any food, then he's going to kill me."

Lucinda snatched Echo's cellphone from her. She texted Devonte that she had been pulled over by the police and she'd hit him back once they let her go. He hit her back, telling her to hurry the fuck up.

"The fuck?" Lucinda said under her breath. "Oh, hell naw, who the hell he thinks this is? I'm 'bouta tell his ass off." She began texting him back, but Olivia snatched the cellphone from her and passed it to Blanca.

"You needa check yourself, Lucinda. You was about to hit her kids' father back with some shit that would possibly get her head knocked off if he's as big of a monster as you claim he is," Olivia stated. She mashed out her joint against the red bottom of her shoe, placed it back inside of the case, and stored it back inside of her handbag.

"Oh, he most definitely is. You'll see." Lucinda assured her. "Echo, show her what you showed the rest of the girls."

Lucinda began rubbing Echo's back comfortingly again. She took a deep breath, unbuckled her belt, and pulled her jeans down below her navel. Above her lips was a branded, cursive, capital

letter D, raised up from her skin like Braille. The girls cringed and looked away when they saw the hideous marking.

"Bitch ass nigga, branded her like she was cattle or some shit," Lucinda said.

"Sick bastard." Olivia shook her head, seeing what had been done to Echo.

"That's not all either. Go ahead, Echo, show them," Lucinda urged her.

Echo cried as she pulled up her jeans and buckled her belt. After she passed Blanca her handbag, she removed her jacket and top. She gave them to Lucinda. Echo was only wearing her bra and jeans now. She spread her arms and turned around in a circle so the girls could get a good look at her. Her body was grotesquely scarred by burn marks, old cuts, welts, and keloids. The sight brought tears to Olivia and Blanca's eyes, but they blinked them back. Lucinda, on the other hand, although she'd already seen her body, let a couple of teardrops fall from her eyes. "You can stop now, mamas." She placed her hand on her shoulder.

"Wait, there's—there's one more thing I'd like—I'd like to show you," Echo told them. The girls exchanged glances, wondering what else she could possibly have to show them.

"Go ahead, Echo. Show us," Olivia encouraged her.

"Okay," Echo replied timidly and brought her trembling hands to the arms of her designer shades. She removed them from her face. The girls gasped and placed their hands over their mouths. Tears burst from their eyes and flowed down their cheeks. Echo's right eye had been plucked out of its socket.

"Jesus Christ! What—what happened, Echo?" Blanca asked.

"We were out to dinner about a year ago when he accused me of looking at the waiter. But I had—had to—to order my food. He—he accused me of flirting with—with him too," Echo explained with an emotionally shaky voice and tears sliding down her left cheek.

She was reliving the awful night her kids' father had maimed and disfigured her. "When we got home, he heated a firewood poker inside of the fireplace until it—until it was glowing orange

and hot. He beat me into submission, and then he—then he—Oh, God—" Echo bowed her head and broke down sobbing. Her head shook, and her shoulders rocked.

Olivia, Blanca, and Lucinda embraced her all at once. Echo's sobbing was so loud and saddening that it drew the rest of the girls from out of the backroom. They all joined in the group hug in support of her. It wasn't long before there wasn't a dry face inside of the bar.

Olivia pulled away from the group wiping the wetness from her eyes. She sniffled before going on to address Echo. "Listen, baby girl. You don't have to rock your baby daddy asleep. I understand your situation. You love that nigga, and he's the father of your children. How about if I come up with a plan that'll get him out the way and allow you to reign over his territory? Would you be willing to sit at the table I've prepared then?"

"Yes, I'd be willing. But only if it doesn't come at the cost of his life." Echo sniffled and wiped her nose with her finger.

"Okay, mama, you've got it," Olivia assured her. She straightened out Echo's crooked wig, took her designer shades from her, and slipped them back onto her face. She hugged the poor girl and motioned for the rest of the girls to join in.

"Yeah, ya wifey loosenin' up, Blakey Boy. Look at her creamin' all over my dick!" Goo glanced down at the creamy lather forming on his piece as he threw himself in and out of Theresa. "When was the last time you dicked this bitch down, bruh? Huh? When the last time you dicked yo hoe down?" he looked over to Blake and pointed his gun at him. The man was beet red, his eyes were glassy pink, and tears were sliding down his cheeks. Globs of yellowish-green snot were hanging out of his nose and down over his top lip. The poor bastard was sobbing and whining like a fifth-grade sissy.

"Tell me before I blow this bitch's head off," Goo snarled, pressing his banga to the back of Theresa's head.

"We—we haven't had sex in years!" Blake sobbed and whined louder.

With his hand over his mouth, Paperchase laughed and shook his head. The ugly faces Blake was making were hilarious to him.

"That's 'cause that lil' pink Willie of yours ain't cutting it, dawg. Yo bitch need some of what I got. Yo bitch needs some of this Mandingo Warrior dick!" Goo looked back at him, smiling wickedly. He loved the fact he was humiliating the man. It was exactly what Scorpion had ordered them to do before they killed his bitch-ass. This was how Hoffa wanted his order executed.

"Aye, Blood, look at him! Look at the homie fuck yo' wife, nigga!" Paperchase barked, seeing Blake squeeze his eyes shut and turn his head. He couldn't bear to watch his wife get violated any further. It was killing him inside. What made it worse was she appeared to be enjoying it. Unfortunately, Paperchase didn't give a fuck what it was doing to him. He was given strict orders, and he was going to carry them out. Paperchase smacked him upside the head a couple of times which seemed to turn him redder. With his gloved hand, he grabbed a handful of hair and pressed his gun into his cheek. "Sit yo ass up and look! Look muthafucka, or I swear I'll blow yo face off!"

Blake peeled his eyes open and forced himself to watch his wife get pounded out. To add insult to injury, she seemed to be enjoying it.

"Oh, my God, Theresa, noooo, nooooo!" Blake sobbed.

"I'm—I'm—I'm sorry, baby. But it—it—it feels so goooood!" Goo's backshots had Theresa's ass hitting high notes like Mariah Carey.

Paperchase smacked him upside the head again and posted back up where he was. He smirked as Blake banged the back of his head against the tabletop over and over again, whining. He shook his head and went back to watching the show.

"Yeah, you lil' bitchez keep playing with y'all pussies. That shit—that shit turning a nigga on," Goo said sensually like he was about to get his rocks off. He tilted his head back, moaning, and lowered his gun at his side. Blake's daughters whimpered and cried while manipulating their clits.

"Jesus—Christ, I'm about to—I'm about to have an orgasm!" Theresa announced with veins bulging on her forehead and neck. Her eyes were shut, her nose was scrunched, and her jaws were clenched. She was ready to explode any second then.

Goo grabbed hold of her long, dark blonde hair and pulled her head back. Gritting, he started piping her down like a maniac. His eyes narrowed into slits, and he groaned lowly. He looked from Theresa to her daughters, who were still pleasuring themselves. The sight really had him going. He could feel the pressure building within his pipe, and he was about to bust.

"Oh, oh, oh, here I—here I cummmmm!" Theresa screamed awfully loud, and her eyes popped open. Her entire body shook, and her essence splashed onto the floor below her. Exhausted, she collapsed on the table with her eyes to their whites and breathing heavily. She reached between her legs and rubbed her clit in a circular motion as Goo continued to beat her sex box up.

Paperchase glanced at the time on his Rollie and looked to Goo. "Say, bruh, you needa gon' head and wrap this shit up."

Goo gave him an understanding nod. He sat his gun upon the table, grabbed Theresa's by her hips roughly, and started banging her back out. "Yeah, nigga, this is payback! This is payback for slavery! The assassination of Martin Luther King, Jim Crow, redlining, all the lil' black boys the jakes done slaughtered out in

107

these streets, and all the destruction you racist, whip cracking, blue-eyed devils have caused worldwide!" Goo's burnt black, flabby, hairy butt cheeks became a blur. He was pounding Theresa so hard and fast. "On gang, this pussy bomb as a muthafucka, Blood! I'ma 'bouta bust all on yo wife's face, Blake, leave her shit real gooey!"

"My nigga!" Paperchase pushed the issue of Goo wrapping up his show.

"I got you, big bruh. Aiight, bitch, get down on yo knees and take it like a champ!" Goo snatched his pipe out of her. He squeezed it tight, so his semen wouldn't prematurely shoot out of his dickhead and forced Theresa down on her knees. He tilted her chin up. She stuck out her tongue and groped her breasts, eager to receive her reward. Goo grunted like an irate caveman pumping his meat. String after string of his warm, creamy white semen spat out of his pee-hole. He painted every inch of Theresa's face white. Now that he was vulnerable, she decided to seize the opportunity to react and possibly save the lives of her family.

"Girls, run!" Theresa shouted to her daughters and punched Goo in his balls. The girls fled towards the basement staircase. Goo, wearing a pained expression, stumbled backwards, holding himself. He and Theresa looked at the gun on the table. They went for it at the same time, but he was closer to it. Before he could grab it, Blake kicked it off the table, and it hit the ground. Theresa took it into both hands, cocked back its hammer, and lifted it as Goo charged at her. The semen plastered on her eyes made it difficult to see, but she wasn't going to let it stop her.

Poc, poc, poc, poc, poc!

Goo staggered backwards with his jeans around his ankles and fell awkwardly to the ground. His eyes were wide, and his mouth was open. He took his last couple of breaths, and then his head fell aside.

Blake's daughters ran towards the staircase, screaming and hollering. The oldest was ahead while the youngest was lagging behind near Paperchase. Paperchase yanked her back into him by her hair, and she screamed. Theresa brought her gun around but

108

still found it a task to see. She couldn't make out where Paper-chase began and where her daughter ended. Paperchase took advantage of the situation. He upped his gun and blew a chunk of meat out the side of her neck.

Blocka!

Theresa dropped the gun and smacked her hand over her spurting neck. She fell to the floor, bucking her eyes. Her mouth moved like a fish out of water and absentmindedly kicking her leg.

"Mommyyyyyy!" Blake's oldest daughter screamed in horror, seeing her mother bleeding out on the floor. She stood at the center of the staircase, trembling while holding her hands over her nose and mouth.

"Mommy!" The youngest daughter cried out for her mother with a tear-drenched face.

"Get down here! Get your skinny ass down here, or baby sis is getting the business next." Paperchase barked harshly at the oldest daughter while holding her at gunpoint. She whimpered with her hands held up, surrendering. She slowly descended the staircase, pleading with him not to hurt her sister.

"Don't you hurt them! Don't you dare hurt them! You god-damn monster or I swear to God Almighty, I'll kill you, you black son of a bitch!" Blake shouted with snot bubbles oozing out of his nose and spit flying from his lips.

"Oh, now you wanna grow a pair of balls, huh? Well, it's just a lil' too fucking late! Nigga, shut yo bitch-ass up!" Paperchase roared with spittle leaping from his mouth. He kicked the table Blake was nailed to so hard, it flipped over and slammed him on his face. He broke his nose and bloodied his mouth.

"Daddyyyyy!" the youngest daughter called out to her father and tried to run to his side. Paperchase yanked her little ass back with so much force her legs went up into the air, and she fell to her knees. She cried out, almost having her hair nearly snatched out of her scalp.

"Shut yo ass up!" Paperchase growled at her. "You, sit over there with your back against that pillar," he told the oldest daughter and motioned her over to the pillar with his gun. She did

exactly like he'd ordered. "Damn, my nigga, Goo." Paperchase closed his eyes momentarily, sucked on his bottom lip, and shook his head. It hurt his heart to see Goo wearing a dead look on his face while lying in his own blood.

Paperchase scanned the basement for something he could bind the sisters' wrists with. His eyes lit up when they came across a red toolbox sitting upon a table among other boxes and miscellaneous items. "Look inside that toolbox and see if there is any duct tape. You pull anything out of there besides what I told you to get, and I'm going to shoot your sister in the face. Do you understand?"

"Yes," the youngest sister whimpered.

Paperchase shoved her forward, but she caught herself before she could fall. She rummaged through the toolbox while he went through some other boxes on the opposite side of the basement. He kept his gun on the oldest sister while performing his search. He smirked when he came across two black pillowcases thinking how perfect they'd be for what he had in mind.

"I—I found the duct tape." The youngest sister sniffled and wiped her snotty nose. Paperchase instructed her to duct tape her sister's mouth and tape her wrists around the pillar. Once she was done, he gave her one of the pillowcases and told her to put it over her head.

"It's going to be okay, alright?" the youngest sister told her older sibling. Tears slid down her cheeks as she nodded in response. Her younger sister kissed her on the cheek and hugged her. Then she pulled the pillowcase over her head and followed Paperchase to the other side of the basement. She sat down with her back against the pillar across from her sister. She cried silently as her wrists were duct-taped around the pillar. Paperchase was about to duct tape her mouth when she looked up at him with pleading eyes. "Are you a—a man of your word?" He nodded. "Well, do you think you can—can promise not to kill me and my sister?"

Paperchase looked over his shoulder at her sister and then back at her, nodding. "You've got my word, shorty. I'm not gon' body you or yo sister."

She sighed with relief, knowing she and her sibling wouldn't be murdered. "Okay. Thank you, thank you, thank you." Her eyes landed on the table he'd kicked over earlier. A look came over her face like she recalled something. "Oh, and my dad, you've gotta promise not to hurt my—mmmummm." Her words were cut short by Paperchase duct taping her mouth shut. He wasn't about to lie to her. Whether she liked it or not, her pops was going wherever he'd sent her mother.

Paperchase pulled the black pillowcase over her head, picked up his gun, and walked over to Blake.

He kneeled down to him and spoke cool and calmly, "That man yo wife laid down was a stalwart soldier, ya heard? He and a few other homies put in the groundwork that laid the foundation of this thing of ours we got going today."

He snorted and pulled on his nose. "My man has two baby mamas and five kids that depend solely upon him to take care of them. Regardless of what I just told your daughter, I'm not leaving y'all here alive without compensation for my nigga's family."

"I've got two hundred thousand dollars inside of my study. It's located inside a digital safe behind the Picasso painting. The combo is 75-85-96," Blake told him as best as he could with a fractured jaw.

Ten minutes later, Paperchase returned to the basement with a lumpy pillowcase and sat it at the end of the staircase. He tucked his gun in his waistband, pulled a hunting knife from the small of his back, and a throwaway cellphone from out of his pocket. He activated the record option and kneeled down to Blake. As soon as he saw the gleaming knife, his eyes bucked. He hollered and struggled to get free of the table he was nailed against.

"Noooo, please, I don't want—I don't want to diiiie, uh, uh, uh!" Blake balled his face up in agony as the hunting knife slammed into his right eye. He tried to reason with Paperchase, but his words fell on deaf ears.

Paperchase yanked his hunting knife out of his eye and went crazy, stabbing him in his face. He slammed the knife into his cheek, nose, mouth, and neck. He closed his eyes as his victim's blood collected on his ski mask. He pulled the knife out of his cheek and wiped away the blood dripping from his mask. When he looked down at Blake, he was staring up at the ceiling with blood pouring out of the wounds in his face. He was dead!

Paperchase stopped the recording, put away the throwaway cellphone, and stood up. He looked at Blake's daughters. They were screaming into the duct tape, squirming around, and kicking their legs. They'd heard him stabbing their father to death and were fearful they were next. Paperchase looked over the bloody mess he'd made of Blake. He picked up the lumpy pillowcase from the bottom of the staircase and walked up the steps.

Chapter 17

Paperchase left Blake's crib to find someplace to discard the gun and hunting knife he'd used in the slayings. He had the Harlem River in mind but decided against driving up there. He and the homies usually discarded weaponry they'd used in crimes and dead bodies they didn't want to be found there. The last thing he wanted was that river to be drained and all they'd disposed of to be recovered and the law coming around asking questions. He'd made up his mind to dump the murder weapons in a location that only he knew about. It was best that way.

Paperchase punched in the address of the location he had in mind in his navigation system. As soon as the automated voice started speaking to him, his cellphone rang from where it was mounted on the dashboard. Seeing who it was, he answered the call and continued to follow the directives the navigation system gave him.

"What's good?" Paperchase asked.

"Shit. Chilling at the house. What you got going, Papi?" Olivia replied.

"I gotta take care of something, and then I'm sliding home, ma. I'm tired as a runaway slave."

"I'm sure I got something that can keep you up. Why don't you come through once you take care of whatever, Papi?" she said, sensually changing the tone of her voice in an effort to seduce him.

"Nah, if bro was to ever find out about us, he'd paint the streets with our blood."

"Nigga, if you're scared, go to church," Olivia told him. He could hear her going through drawers, so he figured she was looking for something.

"Scared? Fuck you talking about? I'm the biggest gangsta in these streets, ma. This whole city is mine. I'm the King of Brooklyn," Paperchase replied with a scowl. Olivia had upset him with that 'scared' shit. She was playing on his ego, but he was too blind to peep game.

"I can't tell."

"What's that supposed to mean?"

"I think you know what it means, gangsta. I mean, Scorpion is calling all the shots from behind the wall, got you niggaz running errands like y'all his flunkies, and to top it off, he basically told you, you bet not dare fuck his pussy," she told him. "I think anyone listening to this conversation would definitely say he's the king of the trenches."

Paperchase was scowling so hard that the vein on his temple looked like it was going to burst. He gritted his teeth and clutched the steering wheel so tight his knuckles turned white. He was seething and ready to explode like a stick of dynamite.

"You got me fucked up; I'm not anybody's flunky! I do whatever I want and fuck whoever I want. That includes you!"

"All I'm hearing is a whole lotta talking, my nigga! You gon' have to show me something!"

"You want me to show you something? Aiight, I'ma show yo ass, on the dead homies!"

"Yeah, whatever," she said.

Then he heard what sounded like hair clippers running.

"What's that?" he asked curiously.

"My vibrator. I want some real dick, but I know yo scary-ass ain't gon' come fuck me, so I guess I'll just have to make do," Olivia told him, playing on his manhood again. "Ooooou! Ooooou! Shhh—shiiiiiit! Ah, fuck, I think—I think I'm about to cum already!"

Urrrrrrrk!

Paperchase whipped his SRT around, leaving tire prints and clouds of smoke into the air. He mashed the gas pedal, the red needle of the speedometer spun, and his car zipped up the street through an intersection. He nearly hit two cars coming from opposite directions, but he didn't give a fuck.

"Uh, uh, uh, uh, uh, yes, yes! Oh, my God, oh my God! I'm about to—I'm about to have an orgasm!"

114

The louder Olivia got, the faster Paperchase drove. He was going so fast that his vehicle looked like a blur flying up the street, leaving debris clouding the air.

Olivia's sexual cries turned Paperchase on so much his dick had bricked and threatened to burst from behind his zipper. He was sure he had cum prematurely because he could feel something slimy and warm against his thigh.

"I'ma show you, shorty! I'ma show you that I'm the king of this shit! This muthafucka right here!" Paperchase claimed, smacking his fist against his chest like a caged guerilla.

"Here it is! Ooooooooooh, shiiiiiiiiii—" Paperchase disconnected the call in the middle of Olivia reaching her orgasm.

Urrrrrrrk!

The SRT fishtailed as he hung a right at the corner and zipped up the block. He whipped by cars lined up on either side of the street. His head was on a swivel as he looked around for Olivia's house. He'd only been there twice, so he didn't know exactly what side of the block it was located, but he knew it once he saw it.

There it is! Right there on the left, Paperchase thought once he saw the two-story, red-bricked house Olivia's grandparents had left her when she passed away.

"All the dirt I done did in the streets, all the penitentiary chances a nigga done took, as many opps the kid done smoked, and you gon' bring that scared shit to me? Okay, you're about to see what's up! I'ma show yo' lil' ass, on gang!" Paperchase drove up into the driveway of Olivia's crib, grabbed his banga, and hopped out, leaving the driver's door open. He ran up the steps of the front porch like he was the fugitive of a nationwide manhunt and pounded on the door like a lunatic. He impatiently tapped his foot and looked around, waiting for her to open the door. Frustrated, he turned to the door again and pounded on it—harder this time.

"Ah, ah, ah, ah, ooooooooou!" Olivia's sexual cries brought his attention around to the bushes. He peered in through the window. She was lying on the couch in her polyester robe. Her legs were wide open, and she had a purple vibrator pressed against her

clitoris. Her eyes rolled to their whites like Satan had suddenly taken possession of her body, and her legs started shaking crazily. Then her toes curled, and a clear liquid sprouted out of her pussy like water from a fountain. Her eyes bucked, and her mouth hung open.

"Open the door up! Open the door!" Paperchase demanded while tapping the butt of his gun against the window. Olivia got up from the couch on wobbly legs letting him see her in all of her glory. She took a step forward and almost fell. That second orgasm had left her freaky ass weak in the knees. She righted herself and walked over to the window. Shorty wore a devilish smile across her face, loving the fact she'd manipulated him into coming over. "Fuck you standing there for? Open the door!"

"Fuck you!" Olivia spat and threw up her middle finger at him. "I'm not opening up shit. If you want this pussy, you gon' have to break this fucking door down and get it!"

Paperchase charged up the steps and rammed the front door with all his might. He ran back to the end of the porch and threw himself into the door three more times. The door rattled from the brute force, and the locks began to tear out from the door frame. His forehead was peppered with sweat, and he was breathing heavily. But he was determined to get that pussy.

Paperchase kicked at the lock of the door with all his might.

Boom, boom, boom, ba-boom!

The door flew open and sent a shard of wood hurling across the living room. Paperchase dropped his banga on the floor and stripped down to his sneakers. He stalked towards Olivia, who was standing behind the couch with her hands on her hips and that same devilish smile on her face.

"You know you done fucked up, right?" Paperchase told her with a frown before grabbing her by her neck roughly. He looked her in the eyes hatefully before tonguing her ass down. Their full lips swept up, down, and side to side as they made out. The sound of the saliva in their mouths filled the living room. Paperchase pinched and pulled on her nipples. Then he began groping her breasts as she tugged on his piece. His pipe grew wider and longer

116

in her grip, and then a slimy, clear-like glob oozed out of its pee-hole.

Paperchase gently bit down on her bottom lip and pulled on it. He then sucked on it while groping her titties like they were two balls of dough. Using his tongue, he traced her jawline, throat, and collarbone and sunk his gold fangs into her neck. Her eyes popped open, and she gasped, feeling him sucking on her like a blood-thirsty vampire. The sensation made her nipples and clit stiffen. She closed her eyes and mouthed 'fuck' over and over again. Her small feminine hands ran up and down his back.

"Papi—Pa—Papi—don't—don't leave any hickies, okay? Scorp—Scorpion will know," Olivia said under her breath.

Paperchase's head snapped upward, and he looked into her eyes. He grabbed her up by her neck again. Only this time, she was standing on her toes. Her eyes rolled again, and she clenched her thighs. The mannish way he handled her nearly made her orgasm for the third time.

"Fuck Scorpion! Brooklyn is mine, and this pussy is mine!" Paperchase talked his shit with mad confidence and grabbed her by her pussy Donald Trump-style. Off but, little mama trembled hard, and her essences poured down her thighs.

"O—Okay, Papi," Olivia said with her eyes still white and her licking her lips.

"Nah, bitch! I wanna hear you say the shit!" Paperchase gave her a little shake, and she gagged. The entire time he was talking to her, he was jacking his dick in preparation to bust her down.

"Brook—Brooklyn is—is yours—and so—so is this—this pussy," Olivia managed to say between breaths.

"That's a good bitch." Paperchase kissed her in the mouth again and then bent her ass over the couch. He hiked up her house robe and kicked her legs apart. He swept his swollen dickhead up and down her dripping slit. He grabbed her by her left shoulder and jammed his pipe up in her. Shorty's eyes bucked, and she gasped.

Yeah, this pussy feels good. This pussy is mine! All mine, Paperchase thought with his eyes closed for the moment as he

117

clenched his jaws. He then started fucking Olivia like a savage beast, ramming his piece up in her hard and fast. His pounding into her globes sent ripples up them. The sound of damp skin smacking against each other filled the air. She was screaming and hollering as he stuffed her fine ass like a Thanksgiving turkey.

"Uh, uh, uh, uh, yes, yes, Papi! Yes, fuck me! Fuck me harder!" Olivia cried loudly. He forced her head down against the backrest of the couch, placed both her hands behind her back, and held them by their wrist. He then grabbed a handful of her hair and yanked it back. She whined like a puppy with her eyes closed. The pain in her scalp from him pulling her hair combined with him dicking her down was what dreams were made of.

Paperchase bit down hard on his bottom lip while fucking the dog shit out of Olivia. The faint scent of their sex manifested in the air, and he loved it. He loved it so much he closed his eyes and inhaled it. Every so often, he'd smack her across both ass cheeks and make them jiggle. It hurt and felt good at the same time, so she encouraged him to do it again. He obliged and kept lapping at her. He became hot and sweaty. Beads of sweat ran down his face, chest, back and disappeared between his hairy buttocks.

"Fuck me, fuck me, Papi! Fuck the shit out of me!" Olivia whined with her eyes squeezed shut and her forehead wrinkled. "Ooooou! I love it! I fucking love it, baby!"

"Unh, huh, unh, huh! Gon' tell me I'm scared? Fuck, you think this is, huh?" Paperchase talked some more of his shit again. He was taking her little mixed ass to Pound-Town, and she loved it. The sounds she was making made his ego swell and soar like a seagull. "Didn't I tell you Brooklyn is mine? And that I'm the king of all this shit? Huh?" *Smack*! He swatted her right buttock, and she hollered.

"Yes, yes, you told me, you told me, baby!"

"I can't fucking hear you!"

Smack!

Paperchase swatted her left buttock.

"Yes, yes, you told me, Pa! I'll never question your status again. Te lo prometo, papi, este coño es todo tuyo! (I promise, daddy, this pussy is all yours!)."

"Oh, yeah, talk that Spanish shit to me, ma! That shit gon' make me nut."

"You gon' bust all in this pussy, Papi?" She looked over her shoulder, throwing that ass back and flicking her tongue at him.

"Yeah, yeah." Paperchase frowned with his eyes closed and tilted his head back. He had both of his hands behind his back like a police officer was handcuffing him. Olivia could tell by the look on his face he was about to bust at any given minute.

"Oh, yeah? You gon' paint my walls with your babies, huh?" She asked. Now she was throwing it back against him faster and faster. He scrunched his nose and clenched his jaws, making them pulsate. "Entra, papi, llena este coñito apretado! (Come in me, Papi, fill this tight, little pussy up!)."

All that dirty talk combined with that WAP pushed Paperchase over the edge. He grabbed her so tight by the waist her meaty hips seeped between his fingers. He slammed himself inside of her down to his dangling nut sack, grunted beastly-like, and emptied his balls inside of her womb. She squeezed her eyes shut, gritted, shrieked, and shook uncontrollably. The feeling of his warm, gooey semen splashing against her eternal walls gave her orgasm number four. Exhausted, she fell over the couch, and Paperchase collapsed on top of her. His eyes were closed, and he was breathing like he'd just run a marathon. Hot beads of sweat slid down his face, arms, legs, and body. Lying there on top of her, he listened to her heart while she felt the rhythm of his against her back.

"That was—that was great," Paperchase spoke of the sex.

"Hey, your majesty, you owe me a new front door," Olivia said, staring at the ruined front door.

Chapter 18

Olivia sashayed out of the bathroom, where she left Paperchase showering. She dried off and tossed her towel aside. Her butt cheeks took turns jiggling with each step she took towards her dresser. She put deodorant under her arms and then grabbed her black bra and panties from out of her top dresser drawer. She put them both on, grabbed the bottle of lotion, and plopped down on the side of her bed. She squeezed lotion into her palm and started rubbing it down her neck, chest, and arms. She was in the middle of applying it to her legs when she heard the dials over the tub twisting. The water spraying from the showerhead stopped. A minute later, Paperchase walked into her bedroom, holding a towel on his waist. His dreadlocks were dripping wet, and his body was covered in beads of water.

"Yo, you got something I can throw on 'til I get home?" Paperchase asked her.

"There are a couple of things of your brother's here. They may fit a lil' big on you, though," Olivia replied.

"I'm not wiggin', I just need something clean to put on for the time being," he told her. "A nigga just took a shower. I'm not trying put back on the same shit I wore over here."

"What I have of your brother's is in the bottom dresser drawer, Papi. Help yourself," she said. Then she went back to applying lotion to her legs.

Paperchase stifled through the bottom dresser drawer until he found something he could wear home. He came up with a wife-beater, an oversized Champion hoodie, and a pair of black denim jeans two sizes too big. He dropped the towel in a pile at his bare feet. He pulled on a pair of socks and stepped into a pair of his brother's Fruit of the Loom boxer briefs. He put the rest of the clothes on but used his own belt to hold up the oversized jeans.

Paperchase threw the hood over his head and tucked his gun in his waistband. He bagged the clothes he'd worn over and threw Olivia the deuce, as he headed towards the door.

"Well, bye to you too, nigga." Olivia grinned from over her shoulder, taking note of how he didn't give her a proper goodbye. She went back to rubbing lotion on her legs and then went down to her feet.

"Fuck!" Paperchase cussed as he recalled something, stopping in the hallway. He walked back inside the bedroom. "Yo, Liv, I need a favor."

Olivia turned around on the bed giving him her undivided attention. "Anything, sweetie."

"I painted a house for bro earlier tonight, but I forgot to take the paintbrushes and shit back to the shed." Paperchase was speaking in a code that he and his circle were very familiar with. She understood he'd chopped some niggaz down, and it had slipped his mind to get rid of the murder weapons.

Olivia shook her head with disappointment. "You're slipping, Papi. I mean really slipping."

"I know. I know." Paperchase nodded as he stared ahead.

I let that tight, wet pussy of hers get in the way of me handling my business. Had Jake pulled me over with that knife and that gun from those murders, they would have been able to trace them back to those bodies back at that bitch ass D.A.'s crib, Paperchase thought and looked over at Olivia, who looked like she wanted to eat him up.

Son, I'ma have to tighten up and really stop fucking with this broad before I end up dead or locked away forever.

Paperchase glanced at the time on his cellphone. "I don't want to be out this late trying to drop everything off, so I was hoping I could leave it here until tomorrow."

Olivia rose from the bed and walked over to him. She grabbed the front of his hoodie, pulled him into her, and tongued him down. She pulled away from him, licking her lips and squeezing his dick through the oversized jeans. "The answer to the question is yes, but I'm going to do you one better, Papi. I'll take them to the shed myself, so you'll have one less thing on your to-do list." She licked the vein on the side of his neck, sunk her teeth into it, and sucked on it like a leech. He closed his eyes, tilted his head

back, and exhaled. While sucking on his neck, she'd slipped her hand inside of his jeans and started jacking his pipe.

"Good—good look—looking out—sh—shorty," Paperchase stammered with his eyes rolled to their whites and his mouth partially opened. The look on his face, coupled with his pleasured moans, gave off zombie vibes.

This shit is too easy. I got this nigga gone off this pussy. In a minute, I'ma have him doing whatever the fuck I please, Olivia thought as she nibbled and sucked on his earlobe.

"One hand washes the other both wash the face. You agree?" Olivia asked between stimulating his earlobe.

"Y—yeah."

"Good. 'Cause in exchange, I want you to let me suck this big, black dick and fuck me like you just came home."

"You got that."

Olivia got down on her knees and hastily unbuckled his belt. The oversized jeans dropped in a heap around his ankles. She pulled down his boxer briefs and came face to face with his one-eyed snake. It was long, thick, hard, and pulsating with a clear, gooey fluid seeping out of its pee-hole. Olivia started massaging his nuts in her palm like they were two metal Baoding balls. She spit on his dick twice, started pumping it while licking around its swollen bulbous head. The sensation sent chills up his spine, and his mouth quivered. Her teasing was driving him crazy. She knew he couldn't wait to feel her hot salivating mouth on the end of his piece, so she took him all the way inside of her mouth. Then she started giving him slow neck, making it sound sloppy and wet.

"Aaaaah, fuck, Blood! Damn, shhhhiiiiit!" Paperchase said, feeling her mouth sliding up and down his pipe. His eyes bucked, and his moaning grew louder and louder. He rose to the tip of his sneakers and grabbed the back of her head. He slapped her hand down and started fucking her mouth without regard. She took his thrusts like a grand champion, showing proof she didn't have a gag reflex. "Shit, I'm about to bust."

Upon hearing that, Olivia popped his dick out of her mouth and wiped her dripping lips. "Nah, not yet. You gon' gimme that

just came home dick first." She stood back up and helped him out of his clothes. They kissed until they reached the bed. He pushed her down, made her assume the doggy style position, and proceeded to give her that just came home dick.

***

Olivia lay naked underneath the sheets with her fist propped underneath her chin. Her hair was disheveled, and a sexually satisfied smirk was on her lips. She watched Paperchase as he sat on the side of the bed, slipping on his oversized jeans and buckling his belt. Once he'd gotten fully dressed, he left the bedroom to retrieve the items he'd used to 'paint the house' with. Paperchase returned with everything wrapped neatly in a sweater.

"Good looking out, ma." Paperchase tried dapping her up.

Olivia looked at him like he'd offered to let her fuck him in the ass. "Niggaaa." She pulled him down by the front of his hoodie and kissed him. They both pulled away, smiling.

"I hope you enjoyed it 'cause that's our last time," Paperchase said, wanting to make things clear.

"Please," Olivia told him with twisted lips and waved him off. She understood that while Paperchase said one thing, his dick said another. His prized pipe belonged to her, and she'd have it whenever she wanted it.

"I'm serious," he said over his shoulder, walking out the door.

"Yeah, I know. Lock my door behind you," she replied. She unwrapped the sweater, revealing a gun and a hunting knife. Smiling devilishly, she wrapped the items back up and tucked the sweater under the side of the bed. She laid back, biting on her pinky nail while staring up at nothing.

I know exactly how I'm going to put these to use, Olivia thought as she picked up her cellphone to make a call.

Chapter 19

"Ramone!"

"Ramooone!"

"Ramooooone!"

The morning sunlight shone on Ramone's face as he lay asleep. His forehead crinkled, and his nose scrunched, hearing his name being called over and over again. His eyes fluttered like the wings of a dying butterfly. Sitting up, he dug the cold out of his eye and looked to Toya's side of the bed. She was gone. In her place, he found the shirt he'd given her last night and a folded sheet of paper with his name written across it.

"Ramooooone, where the hell are you?" Martha shouted as loud as she could. He could hear the chain rattling as she struggled to get free. Still, he knew she was fine, so there wasn't any rush for him to go running to assist her. He planned to holler at her once he saw what Toya had written him.

"Ramoooooone!" Martha shouted again.

Ramone unfolded the letter and read over it:

My dearest Ramone

I cannot thank you enough for last night. I haven't gotten sleep like that in years. I know this may sound corny, but I believe God sent you down from the heavens to watch over me like a guardian angel. I know this sounds crazy, but I literally prayed for someone to love me, protect me, care for me, and treat me like I am someone special. You made me feel all of the above last night. No cap. Ttyl.

XOXO Ms. Toya Miller

A smirk had formed at the corner of Ramone's face once he'd finished reading Toya's letter. He folded it up and placed it inside of his top dresser drawer, where he kept a lot of miscellaneous items. Being as poor as he was, Ramone didn't have a variety to choose from when it came to the opposite sex. The girls at school didn't have much holler for him, given his attire and raggedy

sneakers. The chicks he thought were bad were way out of his league, so he didn't have a chance of scoring with them. That didn't stop him from getting his dick wet, though. He slapped skins with the least favored at his high school: homely chicks, heavy-set girls, and real bony broads.

Having a young lady as attractive as Toya vying for his affection and acceptance had his head in the clouds. It wasn't every day that a guy like him had some eye candy trying to be the girl on his arm. This boosted his confidence and had him walking around with his chest out. He knew for sure once he started making moves with Jabari and them, he was going to be getting bags that would have bitches twice as bad as Toya trying to fuck with him. The thought of it had him envisioning his future and how beautiful it could possibly be.

"Ramone, where the fuck are you?"

"I'm coming, momma! Gimme a second. Goddamn!" Ramone said, slipping his feet into a pair of corduroy house shoes and walking out of his bedroom. He pulled a key out of his basketball shorts, unlocked his mother's bedroom door, and stuck his head inside. She was sitting on the end of her bed, sweaty and disheveled.

"What the hell is this?" Martha held up her shackled wrist.

"A necessary step in guaranteeing you can't escape," he told her. "I know you won't go to rehab on your own, so I decided I'd bring it to you."

"No, baby! No. This isn't the right way to go about this," Martha said with a horrified look on her face. The thought of what was to come from her detoxing had her worried. "I could—I could get so sick from withdraws I could die. I know you don't want your mother to die, do you?"

"Nah. And through the grace of God, you won't."

Martha dropped her head, and her shoulders shook. She broke down sobbing with tears sliding down her cheeks. Sniffling, she looked back up at her baby boy with a soaked face and snot bubbles coming out of her nostrils. She swallowed the spit in her throat. "Ramone, baby, I beg of you, please, don't do this. I'm not

gonna be able to hack it, baby. The stomach aches and nausea are unbearable. I tried to do this before, and I failed miserably."

Ramone looked into the face of his heroin addict of a mother. She looked so sorrowful and weak then. He'd heard countless stories of how painful it was for a junkie to kick their habit, and he didn't want to be the cause of his mother's suffering. He fished the key to the lock of her shackle out of his pocket, and relief spread across her face. He moved to free her from her imprisonment but stopped in his tracks. Her face balled up, wondering what had suddenly come over him.

"What are you waiting for, baby? Turn momma loose," Martha told him, shaking her shackled wrist and causing the chain to rattle.

Ramone stared at the floor like he was thinking something over. He looked back up at his mother and shook his head. He pocketed the key and turned to walk away.

Martha's face contorted into a mask of rage, and her eyes ignited. "Why, you lil' mothafucka, gimme that key!" she ran at him full speed ahead, but he didn't bother turning around. She'd gotten halfway across the bedroom when the chain snagged her back. She was airborne for a moment before she crashed back to the dirty, gum-stained carpet. Holding her aching back, she bawled and cried, watching her son walk out of the bedroom. "Ramone, please, don't do me like this, please! I can't take it! I can't take—"

Martha's pleads were cut short when Ramone slammed and locked the door behind him. He placed his back up against the bedroom door. He leaned his head back against it and closed his eyes. The cries and pleads from his mother were fucking with him mentally, but he knew within his heart that he had to go through with his plan. It was the only way to guarantee that his old bird was going to get clean, and they could be a family again.

"Ramoooooone, baby, I'm begging youuuu!" Martha's voice rang out from behind the door.

Ramone opened his eyes, and hot tears poured out of them. Slowly, he slid down to the carpet, put his knees to his chest, and

wrapped his arms around them. Bowing his head, he continued to listen to his mother while silently crying.

"Ramone, pleeeease!"

After a while, Martha had stopped calling Ramone. He wiped his tear-streaked face with his shirt and got upon his feet. He was heading to the kitchen when he thought he heard a cellphone ringing. He listened closely for it again, and it was coming from his bedroom. That's when he recalled Jabari giving him a cellular so they could keep in contact. With that in mind, he raced into his bedroom and snatched up the pants he'd worn last night. He fished through the pockets until he came up with the iPhone. The letter 'J' was on the screen, so he knew it was Jabari.

"What's the deal?" Ramone answered the call.

"Get dressed, rookie. Today's training day."

***

It was the Haitians versus the Nigerians in a four-on-four game of basketball. The score was 12-8, Haitians. Spectators stood on the sidelines watching the game and reacting to it like they were the gleeful audience at a real-live NBA basketball game, partly due to the fact most of them had some serious bets going on who was to win. Well, it was that and the fact that prison was boring as shit, and any time some real action got going, it had everyone's undivided attention.

Hoffa bounced the basketball as he walked from the opposite side of the basketball court. The sweat covering his face and body twinkled like broken glass below the shining sun. Hoffa adjusted his gold-framed round lens eyeglasses as he made his way down the court towards a Nigerian man. He was about the same size as him. The only difference was his 12 o'clock midnight complexion, bald head, and wide, flat nose. He had his arms spread and his legs wide open, watching Hoffa like a hawk would his prey from the sky.

Hoffa came up to the Nigerian dribbling the basketball between his legs. He was moving so swiftly his salt, and pepper dreadlocks

bounced up and down. He faked left, then right, and then he hit the Nigerian nigga with a vicious crossover.

He made his way down the asphalt with his dreadlocks floating behind him, taking long strides. On his third step, he pushed off the ground, descended into the air, and brought the basketball with him. He took the basketball into both hands and slammed it inside of the basket. Holding onto the rim, he rocked back and forth for a minute. Then he dropped down to his bending knees with the basketball landing behind him shortly thereafter.

"That's game!" Hoffa told the shot-caller of the Nigerians who looked both ashamed and angry. The shot-caller, who was a shorter man with beaded hair and full lips, extended his hand in a show of good sportsmanship. Hoffa arrogantly strolled right past him, leaving him feeling embarrassed and stupid. Hoffa wiped his sweaty face with the lower half of his shirt and wiped clammy hands on it as well. His teammates approached, exchanging pleasantries and shaking up with him. One of his men standing on the sidelines tossed him his uniform shirt; he slipped it on and walked towards Scorpion, who was standing off to the side. The brolic brown skinned man stood at the forefront of a handful of his Woo niggaz. They all wore mean mugs and appeared ready for war if anything jumped off. This was why Scorpion kept these savage animals with him almost everywhere he traveled within the prison. The way he looked at it, the President had his secret service, and he had his—and his was the Woo.

"Good game, my brother," Scorpion told Hoffa as they engaged each other. Hoffa was buttoning the last buttons of his uniform shirt. He also had a handful of savage animals he was at the forefront of. They all looked to be as serious and as dangerous as the niggaz Scorpion was with.

"Thank you, brother. Peace." Hoffa replied.

"Peace." Scorpion said back.

They shook up, hugged, and touched each other's shoulders with their chins three times like they always had in greeting.

"You recall that business we discussed?" Scorpion asked him in a hushed tone.

"Indeed."

"Well, I've got something I'd like you to see—privately."

Right off, Hoffa understood what he was getting at and turned around to his savages. While he exchanged hushed words with them, Scorpion held up his hand, signaling to his beasts to fall back. Hoffa turned around, giving Scorpion a slight nod, and then threw his head towards the track. Scorpion walked up beside him, and they walked over to the track. They quietly trekked around it until Scorpion broke the silence.

"The deed is done. I figured you'd want more than just my word for it, so I went the extra mile to get you proof." Scorpion told him. He took a cautious look around before producing the contraband cellphone he had hidden on him. He pulled up the proof of the kill Paperchase had collected and allowed Hoffa to view it while he watched their backs. For the first time since they'd been locked up, Scorpion saw the Haitian shot-caller smile. He put all thirty-four teeth on display and even chuckled a little.

"Mwen te di ou mwen ta jwenn ou, ou kochon mèrdik. Se pou ou repoze nan kaka ou bèt sal." (I told you I'd get you, you fucking pig. May you rest in shit, you filthy animal). Hoffa spat hatefully in Haitian Creole. He harped up a big nasty glob of mucus, spit on the ground, and started kicking dirt at it. Scorpion wasn't for sure, but he gathered he was imagining himself spitting on Blake's dead body and kicking it mercilessly. "Please, excuse my behavior, brother, but I hated that dick sucka."

"It's all good, brother. I understand," Scorpion assured him and tapped him on his back. He deleted the proof from the cellular, made sure no one was watching him, and then he put the phone back where he had it hidden. He made a mental note to destroy it as soon as possible, knowing it still contained the proof of the murder.

Scorpion didn't know what the hell transpired between Hoffa and Blake to make him despise him so much. And as curious as he was to know he wasn't going to fix his mouth to ask. His beef was his business and his business alone. Hoffa upholding his end of the agreement was what he was concerned with.

"You kept your end of our agreement, so it's only fair that I keep mine," Hoffa told him as he removed his eyeglasses, fogged them with his hot breath, and cleaned them with the end of his shirt. He slipped them back on as he and Scorpion continued around the track.

"Give me a few days. I'll get into contact with my people on the outside and see to it that you get the information you desire. You have my word." He turned to him, looked him in the eyes, and extended his hand. Scorpion made a note of the seriousness in his eyes before shaking up with him. The men went on walking around the track, chopping it up, while their respective killaz watched them from afar.

Ghost & Tranay Adams

Chapter 20

Ramone gripped a long black gun as he hauled ass across the graveled ground. Sweat was pouring down his back, and his face was shiny from perspiration. He was hot, sticky, and tired, but he didn't dare stop for fear of being shot. Ramone glanced over his shoulder and saw two of the shooters coming at him. They were wearing protective headgear with face shields, full tactical body armor, and guns as big, long, and black as the one he was caring for.

Ramone huffed and puffed as he ran, zig-zagging to avoid the projectiles flying all around him from his back. He'd already successfully taken out two of the shooters, and now he had three more he had to dispatch—if he hoped to survive the day.

Pop, pop, pop, pop!

More projectiles zipped around Ramone and splattered against the graffiti-covered warehouse ahead of him. His eyes bucked, realizing how close he'd come to getting taken off his feet.

"Holy shit, son! That was close!" Ramone said to himself. He glanced over his shoulder again and saw the shooter quickly closing the distance between them. He knew that coming so close to taking him out of the game had heightened their egos to astronomical levels.

Niggaz got me running and ducking like some bitch! There ain't no ho in my blood, I'ma make these niggaz respect my G, Ramone thought as his face balled up angrily and his top lip peeled back in a sneer. He disappeared inside of the warehouse, with the shooters coming in shortly behind him.

The two shooters, Boobie and Durty, crept inside of the warehouse. They looked around cautiously while swaying their guns from left to right. The tenement reeked of piss, shit, and mold. It would have been quiet if it wasn't for the brown water dripping from the leaky ceiling and splashing into the scattered puddles on the graveled ground.

"Yo, you see that lil' nigga, fam?" Boobie whispered to Durty.

"Nah, but when I see youngin', I'm taking son head off. That's my word." Durty replied as they crept around the grimy empty building, with their backs to each other.

"If this lil' fucka, ain't on the ground level, then he must be—" Boobie looked above to see Ramone in midair. "Oh, shit!" he scowled, pointed his gun up at him, and rapidly fired.

Pop, pop, pop, pop!

Durty joined in on the action.

Pop, pop, pop, pop!

Ramone managed to avoid getting hit and landed on Durty's shoulders. He upped his gun and struck Boobie twice in his chest. As Boobie hurled backwards, he took one more shot in his face shield. He collided with the graveled ground at the same time Durty did. The impact from the fall knocked the gun free from Durty's gloved hand, and it spun around in circles across the surface. Ramone rolled off of him. When he came back up, Durty was reaching for the gun he'd lost, but he already had the drop on his ass.

Pop, pop!

Durty took two projectiles to the chest, and a third one launched his head backwards. Hearing movement from above, Ramone looked up to see a fifth shooter dressed like the rest of the ones he'd dispatched. He'd upped his long black gun and dumped it at him.

Pop, pop, pop, pop, pop!

Ramone ran away from the rapid gunfire, dove, tuck, rolled, and snatched up Durty's gun while in motion. He came back up on his knees with both guns aimed up at the shooter busting at him from the gallery. He fired the twin weapons in sync.

Pop, pop, pop, pop, pop, pop!

The shooter took all six to his chest, flipped over the guardrail, and plummeted towards the ground. He lost his gun in the freefall and landed on the filthy mattress below. Ramone tossed his empty gun aside as he speed-walked over to the fallen shooter. He stood over him with his own gun and fired twice into his face shield.

Ramone lowered his gun and stood over him, looking over his handiwork. He breathed heavily, with his chest swelling and deflating. He removed his headgear and tossed it aside.

The shooter that had landed on the mattress started clapping his hands in reaction to his performance.

"Good job, yo. Good fucking job." Jabari praised Ramone's performance and sat up on the mattress. He extended his gloved hand up at Ramone as the two shooters the young nigga had taken out earlier entered the warehouse. They had blue paintball splatters on their face shields and tactical body armor as well. "Help me up, dog."

Ramone pulled Jabari up to his feet, and they shook up. Jabari removed his headgear and tucked it under his arm. He patted Ramone on his shoulder and shook it. "I'm proud of you, son. You did your thang today," he told him with a smile.

The two shooters, Boobie and Durty, all removed their blue paintball splattered headgear as they approached Ramone and Jabari. These four men were who Jabari fucked with the hardest out of the Woo. He trusted this quartet of killaz with his life and considered them family within the family. They all went through this same training along with other prerequisites before they eventually earned their Modus operandi.

"You showed up and showed out, son, for real for real." Boobie shook up with Ramone. Durty and the other shooters shook up with him and gave him his props too. Ramone tried not to smile from the praise he was given, but it was hard not to.

"Word to mine, my young nigga a regular chip off the old block," Jabari said with his arm around Ramone's shoulders. "Hard to believe mop-top here hasn't been busting his gun with the accuracy he displayed today." He laughed as he ruffled Ramone's dreadlocks. The young nigga pulled away from him. Jabari threw down his headgear, and they threw playful punches at each other.

Jabari threw Ramone in a headlock and rubbed his knuckles at the top of his head. They joked and laughed heartily.

135

"Yo, son, let's go get cleaned up," Jabari told everyone. "We gon' hit the set tonight. Food and drinks on yo boy." He pressed his gloved hand to his chest.

Jabari and his crew of money-hungry savages ate and drank at David Busters. They talked, joked, laughed, and popped shit at each other, behaving like some fraternity kids on a Saturday night. Jabari paid the bill and dropped a nice tip for the pretty waitress he'd been flirting with since they were shown their table. With that, the homies decided to spend the rest of their night at a gentlemen's club in Manhattan that was growing in popularity.

Jabari sped through the streets with the cool, stale air blowing in through the windows ruffling him and Ramone's clothing. The streetlights flickered on and off their faces as he drove. Jabari looked back and forth between the windshield and Ramone. The young nigga's face was a mask of concentration as he read over the pages of the book that he'd given him as part of his training. The book showed the ins and outs of a man's body, breaking down the human anatomy. It presented over one thousand ways to kill someone effectively, as well as how to paralyze them.

Ramone had been reading the book for the past couple of days. He couldn't help thinking how wicked the man must have been who'd written it. He knew without a doubt it was a man because only a man could sit down and think of so many ways to kill his brethren.

Ramone glanced at Jabari and nudged him, flashing him a page of the book he was reading. "Yo, B, you can't tell me a white nigga ain't put this shit together."

"Oh, yeah? What makes you say that?" Jabari asked with a smirk.

"Look at the history of the Caucasoid, my G," Ramone replied. "The white man's culture is rooted in death and destruction. Yet our people are the ones the world is taught to fear."

Jabari nodded his understanding. "What can I say? When you're right, you're right, Farrakhan."

Ramone grinned and went back to studying his book. Jabari made a couple of stops before the destination they had in mind. He

stopped by his place, where he and Ramone showered and picked out something to wear for the night. Jabari let the little nigga choose whatever he wanted to wear from his wardrobe. He settled on an orange camouflage bucket hat, matching fatigues, and butter Timbs. Jabari decided on some Versace shades, silk gold and black Versace button-up and black Versace loafers with the gold medusa heads. To set his fit off, he threw on his gold Cuban link chain with the Jesus piece and his plain-face gold Rolex watch.

"What up, king? How you liking how ya boy styling and profiling?" Jabari smiled and struck a gang of photogenic poses. His drip was heavy and worthy of a red-carpet appearance.

"You're fresh to death, my G. But I saw something inside yo closet that would really set yo shit off. Gimme one second, son," Ramone ducked off inside of the walk-in closet and came back with a sleek black cane with a stylish gold handle. It looked like it was handcrafted for an ancient Egyptian Pharaoh.

Jabari smiled hard as hell seeing the cane. He took it from Ramone and struck some more poses with it. "What up, kid? How a nigga look?"

"That muthafucka drippy, son. On everything I love," Ramone replied with his arms folded across his chest, taking him in from head to toe.

"Yeah, I like this shit too," Jabari said, looking himself over in the full-body mirror. "They probably won't let a nigga in with this bitch, but it's worth a try, though. Good looking out, my nigga." He shook up with Ramone and playfully smacked his back.

Chapter 21

Jabari and the fellas took Ramone to this new gentlemen's club called Off The Wall. Ramone was far too young to get in, but a hundred bucks made the doorman look the other way. The homies were fascinated by the skimpily dressed beauties walking around, giving a lap dance, or working the pole. The lights were out inside the establishment, so the strippers' neon outfits, glitter, and face paint glowed in the dark, making them look like the characters in the Tron movie.

Ramone was rubbing his hands together greedily while feasting his eyes on the tits and ass coming back and forth across his line of vision. Jabari threw his arm around his shoulders and followed his eyes. He had a grin on his lips, seeing how anxious Ramone was to get into the mix of things.

"I'ma show you how Woo do it. It's all on me tonight, king. Pick any bitch in here you want, and she's yours," Jabari assured him.

"What? You for real?" Ramone asked with a serious expression.

"Nah, for fake. Of course, for real," Jabari told him. "Couple of things you should know about me, son. I don't play when it comes to money, my reputation, and my niggaz. Playing with any of those is liable to get yo wig blown off, ya dig?" Ramone nodded his understanding. "Good. Now scope out these hoes and see which one you want. I'ma have the homies do the same while I secure the VIP section and a few of them gold bottles."

"I want her," Ramone told him, nodding to the stripper he wanted to bust down.

Jabari looked in the direction he was standing in and was surprised by the woman he saw. She was a five-foot-ten light-skinned broad with auburn hair styled in a Mohawk. She had hazel-green eyes and freckles covering her face. Baby was as thick as a Brick Shit House and had an ass as wide as a dump truck. Her 36 Double Ds were spilling out the top of her pink bikini top. Her Daisy Dukes were unzipped to showcase her bald mound. Her meaty

buttocks were three shades darker than her complexion and hung out the bottom of her shorts. When Ramone spotted her, she was in the middle of giving some nerdy-looking white boy wearing bifocals and a pink polo shirt a lap dance. Dude looked like he couldn't handle that great big old ass in his lap. Hell, one of little mama's thighs appeared to be bigger than him.

"My young nigga, now I don't know if you're blessed with the right equipment to tackle all that ass. However, you're Woo material, so I'm sure you'll rise to the occasion," Jabari assured him and hung his arm around his shoulders. Using the hand that held his brick of money, he motioned the BBW over to him. The entire time she'd been giving the nerdy dude his money's worth in lap dances, she'd been seducing Ramone with her eyes and long frog-like tongue. It was safe to say she had the youngster under her hypnosis.

Shorty finished her lap dance, folded up the money she'd collected from old boy, and stuffed it inside of her bikini top. She slid her large acrylic nailed hand down the side of his face and underneath his chin as she walked away. The nerdy white dude sat up in his chair adjusting his eyeglasses and watching her walk away. Her big globes swung from left to right with every step she took. No longer able to control his sexual urges, the nerdy white dude speed walked to the men's restroom to whack one out.

"What up? I'm Jabari. This is my lil' bro, Ramone. What's your name, ma?" Jabari inquired.

"Everyone calls me Boomshakalaka." She leaned forward, shaking her basketball-sized breasts in Ramone's face and that gigantic ass of hers. Ramone seemed to be enticed by her assets. She was strapped, thick in all of the right places. He loved a big, beautiful woman. The young homie didn't discriminate at all.

"Well, Boomshakalaka, my lil' bro likes what he sees, and me being his big brother and the money man, I'd like to see to it that he has a good time. If you know what I mean." Jabari winked at her, and she smirked.

"Oh, I know exactly what you mean," Boomshakalaka said with her eyes on Ramone licking her big juicy lips. She was

looking at him like she was a hungry lioness, and he was an unsuspecting antelope.

"Good. So, how much for the full experience?" Jabari asked her.

"Two bandz, and I'll take him on a trip around the world he'll never forget," Boomshakalaka swore. She gripped the bulge in Ramone's jeans, and he grunted. Her eyes bucked, seeing that he was working with something.

"I got you, ma." Jabari licked his thumb and counted up her fee. She folded it up and slipped it inside of her bikini top.

"You strapped my nigga?" Ramone shook his head. Jabari pulled out two golden foil Magnum condoms and discretely slipped them to him. He patted him on the back and told him to have fun.

"Oh, I intend to," Ramone said happily and shook up with him.

"Come on, baby." Boomshakalaka grabbed Ramone by his hand and led him up the spiral staircase, where all of the real action took place.

"Take it easy on her, king!" Jabari called out to Ramone. He looked over his shoulder and gave him a thumb up before disappearing down the hallway.

Once he'd procured a couple of more strippers for the rest of his homies, Jabari waved down a strapped white girl. She had gray eyes and blonde hair she wore braided in a ponytail. She was wearing a black bikini and matching stilettos. Her eyes got as big as baseballs when she saw the brick of blue faces in his hand. She'd already made up her mind she was going to do whatever she had to do to guarantee she'd leave with at least half of it. Jabari whispered something in her ear, she nodded, and he dropped a few thousand dollars on the tray she was carrying. When she turned to walk away, Jabari smacked her on her ass and watched it jiggle. She looked over her shoulder at him, smiled, and made her booty dance. She then went on about her business.

A few minutes later, Jabari was escorted to the VIP section by a six-foot-tall black girl who was more strapped than the white

girl. She was wearing a leopard ears headband, a two-piece leopard jumpsuit with matching tail, and thigh-high black leather hooker boots. She was a very voluptuous woman with a booty like a filly. As soon as Jabari saw her, he wanted to slap on a cowboy hat, throw a saddle on her and ride her big ass. Once Jabari was seated on the black leather sofa, the black girl placed five golden bottles of Ace of Spades on the table before him. He folded up a one-hundred-dollar bill, motion for the black girl to bend down, and then he tucked it between her breasts. She smiled at him and revealed a mouthful of shiny braces. She tucked the golden platter under her arm and made her way out of the section.

Jabari reached into the front of his jeans like he was Al Bundy and pulled out half a pound of Hawaiian Purple Kush. He'd copped it and a pack of Backwoods on the way over. He got right to work busting up the blunt and filling it with marijuana. When he was done, he had a blunt big enough to make Bob Marley proud. He put fire to the tip of it until it turned into a cherry, took a couple of puffs, and blew out a cloud of smoke. He put out the sparkler on one of the golden champagne bottles and popped it open. Switching hands with the wafting blunt, he took the champagne to the head, guzzling it.

Jabari alternated between smoking and drinking while taking in the scenery of the club. He motioned for what he deemed were some of the finest looking big titty, big booty bitchez over into the section he'd purchased for the night. The females were contemplating whether they should entertain his company or not until they saw the waitress who he'd dropped a few racks on walking toward him. Little mama had two huge blocks of neatly stacked and secured one-dollar bills. Two physically fit men dressed in black caps and black T-shirts with Security sprawled across them flanked her. They were a couple of serious-looking men who had mace and retractable batons attached to their utility belts.

One of them unhooked the velvet rope of the VIP section so the waitress could walk through while the other stood guard in case niggaz was on some bullshit. The waitress entered the section with the vixens. Jabari called over behind her. The women

crowded around him. Two of them sat on his lap, fondling him and whispering nasty things in his ears while the one behind him massaged his shoulders. The waitress who'd brought in the huge blocks of money pushed the gold champagne bottles aside on the table and sat the blocks down upon them. She tore away the plastic wrapping from the blocks and left them stacked neatly on the table before Jabari. She balled up the torn plastic into a ball. He gave her a hundred-dollar bill, which she pocketed, and then took her leave.

Ghost & Tranay Adams

Chapter 22

Jabari had never been the flashy type. He considered his stunting this night as a business expense. He was showing Ramone how the team loved to ball out and have themselves a good time. He figured once the young nigga had gotten a taste of the lifestyle afforded to the Woo, he'd never want to be a lone wolf again.

Jabari was feeling like the boss of all bosses surrounded by all of those beautiful women. He was throwing dollars like they were a pile of leaves while the girls were popping their asses and shaking their titties. A while later, he excused the ladies from his section and slumped down on the sofa. His eyes were low, glassy, and red as he took swigs from the golden bottle. A smirk formed at the corner of his lips when he saw Ramone, Boobie, Durty, and the rest of the crew making their way down the spiral stairs, with the strippers they'd ducked off with following behind them. The strippers went their separate ways while the homies fell in step to the section Jabari reserved.

All the homies shook up with Jabari, grabbed a bottle of their own, and plopped down in their respective seats. Ramone sat across from Jabari, nursing a flute of bubbly with a big ass smile on his face. Jabari smiled, knowing his little homeboy had a ball. It was written all over his face, and he wanted the dirty details. He motioned Ramone over to him, and the young nigga pointed a finger to his chest. He then looked around like he didn't know he was talking to him.

Jabari cupped his hand around his mouth and called out to Ramone. "Stop playing, son, and bring yo' lil' ass over here!"

Ramone laughed, smacked his thigh, and plopped down on the sofa beside him. He downed what was left of his champagne and held his flute towards Jabari. Jabari took the liberty to refill it and passed it back to him. He hung his arm around the young nigga's shoulders, drunk from the bottle of champagne, and listened to him relay his experience with Boomshakalaka.

"Say, bruh, this is by far the greatest night of my life, and all the thanks goes to you. I love you, my nigga. No homo," Ramone said.

Jabari laughed and shook up with him. "I love you too, my young nigga."

Suddenly, the vibration of his cellphone stole his attention. He held up one finger so Ramone would give him a minute, sat his bottle of Ace on the table, and pulled out his cellphone. Sanka was on its screen. Looking over his shoulder, Ramone looked between the name of the person calling him and the perplexed look on Jabari's face. It was like he was trying to decide if he should answer the call or not.

Fuck it. I'm not about to let this nigga ruin the night with talk of business, Jabari thought and declined the call. He then slipped his cellphone back inside of his pocket.

"Yo, everything good?" Ramone asked with a concerned look.

"Oh, yeah. Everything Gucci, just a slide trying to hook up and shit." Jabari lied. "But these hoes, though. I'm trying to tame something new, ya heard?" he held out his fist.

Ramone nodded in agreement and dapped him up.

"Yo, King, you see something else you feeling? If so, lemme know. I got chu. It's all on me," Jabari assured him, switching hands with the bottle and smacking the blocks of money laid out on the table.

"Fa sho." Ramone nodded.

Jabari sprung to his feet and nearly fell. He was so fucked up. He upped his golden bottle and called in the fellas, motioning over in a huddle. "Everyone, I'd like to propose a toast to the gang, long live the Woo!" he threw up his bottle. Boobie, Durty, and the rest of the homies threw up their bottles. Ramone snatched up a bottle from the table and threw up his alongside the others.

"Long live the Woo!" the men said altogether, clinked their golden bottles, and took a drink from them. Unbeknownst to them, two men were watching them from a shadowy area of the club. They'd been scoping them for so long the ice in their glasses of dark liquor melted. Once the men had seen enough, they aban-

doned their watered-down drinks and vanished without their charge ever noticing them.

***

Jabari and the homies left Off The Wall drunk and high out of their minds. The fellas were trying to hit up this after-hours spot, but Ramone wasn't down. He opted to be taken to a 24-hour bodega not too far from the projects to get a few groceries before being taken home. He got exactly what he wanted from the corner market before he was dropped off in Red Hook. He shook up with Jabari and made his way toward his tenement.

Ramone was so inebriated it took him twenty minutes to finally unlock his apartment's door. He locked the door behind him and carried the bags towards the kitchen. He took an awkward step and fell to the floor, spilling some of the contents of his bags.

"Goddamn it!" Ramone cussed. It took a few tries, but he finally got back on his feet. He gathered all the items he'd spilled and placed them back inside the bags. He was entirely too drunk to put everything up, so he just left the bags on the table. Heading to his mother's bedroom, he snatched off his bucket hat and pulled off his polo shirt. He knocked on the door and listened for a reply, but he didn't get one. Figuring Martha was asleep, he went to his bedroom and tossed his bucket hat and shirt aside. He then dove upon his mattress and lay on his stomach until he drifted off to sleep.

***

The murders that transpired at the Kavanaugh's were all over the news, and Paperchase's jack was going bonkers with calls from Goo's baby mamas. He knew they had a million and one questions for him, but they would have to wait until he saw his fence. He was going to keep whatever profits he received from selling Blake's jewelry and throw Goo's baby mamas the loot he'd gotten out of the safe. Normally he'd bust everything down the middle, but Goo had kids, and he wanted to make sure his family was taken care of.

Paperchase was a hundred bandz richer by the time he left his fence. He felt fortunate that both of Goo's baby mamas got along because that meant they could be in the same room with each other. He hit up Brielle and JaJa and made arrangements for them to link up at her crib. They both tried to get him to tell them what had happened to Goo, but all he said was that he heard he'd been murdered during a home invasion, which was the same thing the news had reported.

When Paperchase got to Brielle's crib, JaJa's car was already there. He took a deep breath and knocked on the door. As soon as Brielle opened the door, he was smacked in the face by the unmistakable smell of Ganja and the sounds of Nina Simone. Though the lighting was dim, from over Brielle's shoulder, he could see JaJa sitting on the couch. Shorty wore her hair in a fade with abstract designs cut on the sides. Her high cheekbones, wide pierced nose, full lips, and shapely body made her worthy of designer magazine ads. Every time Paperchase saw Goo's baby mamas, he wondered how he'd managed to get between their legs. Neither of the women were fairly attractive, while Goo, God bless his soul, had a face only a mother could love.

JaJa's eyes were shut as she nodded her head to the music while nursing a glass of red wine. A bottle of Cabernet Sauvignon was on the coffee table alongside a glass of wine. It was clear the ladies had a vibe going.

"What's up, B?" Paperchase greeted Brielle.

"What's up, bro?" Brielle took the joint out of her mouth and hugged him with one arm. She kissed him on his cheek and motioned for him to come inside. When she locked the door behind him, the sound of the clicking brought JaJa out of her zone. She sat up and placed her glass of wine on the coffee table. In the dim lighting, Paperchase could see she'd been crying. Her eyes were red and dry tears were on her cheeks.

"JaJa, what's up, ma?" Paperchase asked with a smirk, trying to sound upbeat, giving the circumstances.

JaJa looked at the troubled look in his eyes and the duffle bag in his hand. Goo had always said if something ever happened to

him, Paperchase would drop some money on her and Brielle to make sure they were taken care of. Tears burst from JaJa's as she shrieked and pressed her hands against her face. She dropped to her knees. Her shoulders rocked back and forth as she grieved heavily.

"He's dead. He's dead! Oh God, it's really true!" JaJa said, devastated. She performed like one of her twin sons had been gunned down in a drive-by.

Brielle turned on the lights and killed the music. She mashed out her joint inside the ashtray on the coffee table and tended to JaJa. Teary-eyed, she held JaJa in her arms and rubbed her back soothingly.

"Shhhhh. It's going to be okay. We're gonna make it through this. You, the kids, and I are gonna make it through this." Brielle sniffled and blinked back tears.

Chapter 23

Paperchase separated the money he'd stolen from Blake's safe into two neat piles on the kitchen table. He leaned back in his chair, popped a Xanax that Brielle had given him from Goo's personal stash, and chased it down with some Dirty Sprite. JaJa had been so heartbroken and distraught over Goo, Brielle was afraid she was going to have a nervous breakdown. Her eyes had swollen so badly she looked like she'd had an allergic reaction to seafood. Luckily, Brielle was able to calm her down. She got her to drink some apple cinnamon tea and take two Tylenol PMs so she could get some sleep. Ten minutes later, shorty was knocked out on the couch. Brielle draped a blanket over her and excused herself to take a shower.

Paperchase sat up in his chair when he saw Brielle stroll out into the living room with a bottle of something in her hand. She was wearing a silk gold and navy-blue Kimono robe with a winged, fire-breathing dragon illustration on the back of it. Her usually long hair had shrunk and curled up thanks to the steaming hot water. Paperchase licked his shiny gold Paperchase and bit down on his bottom lip. His thug ass couldn't stop thinking about all the freaky shit he'd like to do to her.

Brielle was honey complexioned, with an hourglass shape and tattoos covering nearly every inch of her body. Her titties were as big as birthday balloons, and she had enough ass to feed those South African kids with flies stuck to their faces in those old infomercials. Paperchase had always wanted to hit that pussy like a home run in the ninth inning, but she was the homie, Goo's, baby mama. Therefore, she was off-limits.

"Damn, all this is for us and the kids?" Brielle asked, picking up one of the stacks of dead faces and examining it.

Paperchase nodded and relit the joint she had smashed out earlier. He took a couple of pulls from it and blew out a cloud of smoke. Brielle tossed the stack of money back upon the pile she'd taken it from and pulled a chair out from the table.

"Y'all gotta hunnit and fiddy geez a piece. I know y'all gon' trick some of that on y'all selves which is aiight by me, just as long as the majority of that goes to bruh's lil' ones," Paperchase told her and took a couple more pulls from the joint.

"Mommy comes last. I'ma take care of my babies first. Besides, their daddy would have wanted it that way," Brielle replied. He nodded with understanding. "Look, can you do me a favor before you go?"

"What's that, shorty?"

"Lotion my legs for me. I pulled a muscle wrestling with the boys earlier, and now my back is killing me." Brielle handed the pink bottle of Johnson & Johnson to him and put her pretty toes on the chair. Paperchase could see she wasn't wearing any panties. Her coochie was bald, meaty, and its thick clit stuck out like a toddler's thumb. Paperchase thought about bending her over the table full of money and giving it to her long and hard. He quickly shook the thought from his head, though. He already fucked up with his brother behind Olivia. He couldn't do his nigga, Goo, like that. He had to learn to control himself and exercise some dick discipline.

"Fa sho," Paperchase replied.

"Thanks, bro," Brielle took the joint from him and took a couple of pulls from it. Paperchase squeezed some lotion into his palm, rubbed his hands together, and applied the lotion to her leg. He started at her foot, went between her toes, around her ankles, up her calf, and worked his way down her thigh. He went further and further up her thigh. The closer he got to her pussy, the warmer it got. He looked up at her face, and her eyes were squeezed shut, and she was licking her lips. He glanced down at her lower lips, and they were running with her glistening essence.

Paperchase became aroused, and his piece began to stir in his jeans. His dick was so hard, and he could have used it for a harpoon. He tested his limitation by getting closer to Brielle's sex. Her moaning slowly grew louder, and the leg she'd placed on the chair gradually began to tremble. When Paperchase brought his hand up towards her pussy again, she grabbed his hand and placed

it on top of it. Against his better judgment, he slipped two of his fingers inside of her. He worked his digits in and out of her pink while using his thumb to stimulate her clitoris.

"Uh, uh, uh, uh," Brielle tilted her head back and popped her titties out of her bathrobe. She groped them erotically while sucking on their nipples. Paperchase unzipped his jeans and pulled out his thick, vein-riddled dick. He stroked his piece up and down with his right hand while using his left hand to pleasure her.

"Fuck, Blood, I'm horny as hell, yo. I want some of this pussy," Paperchase said loud enough for only them to hear.

"Well, come get it, Pa. Come get yo pussy," Brielle replied, still holding the joint between her fingers. It had burned so far down that its ashes were about to break and fall.

"What about JaJa?" Paperchase asked, looking toward the couch.

"What about her? She's asleep. Now come on, I know you want this pussy." Brielle smacked the piles of money off the tabletop and sent loose dollars in the air. She hiked her bathrobe around her waist, bent over the table, and spread her buttocks wide open. Looking over her shoulder, she teasingly licked her pierced tongue at Paperchase and made her asshole wink at him. Paperchase dick jumped, seeing her crinkle winking at him and entrance to her pink tunnel.

"Damn, that ass and that pussy fat, yo!" Paperchase lustfully eyed her assets. He then smacked her on each of her buttocks. She moaned and shook her butt. "On the gang, shorty, I'm about to fuck the shit out yo ass. Word to the dead homies!" he pulled off his shirt and hoodie all at once and tossed them on the chair he was sitting on. He got down on his knees behind Brielle, spread her ass cheeks apart, and spat on her asshole twice. He licked, sucked on it, and ate it while fingering like a mad man. She made an ugly face, whined, and tilted her head back. Her legs began to shake as he devoured her jewel. Her whining was becoming so loud that JaJa frowned and shifted in her sleep.

Paperchase stood up, wiping his shiny mouth with the back of his fist. He pulled Brielle into him, pressed his hand against the

center of her back, and told her to arch her back. She parted her legs as far as she could and tooted her booty. She licked her top row of teeth and wagged her bodacious ass. Shorty was starving for the dick and couldn't wait to get it.

Paperchase spat in his palm and used his saliva to lubricate his dick. He stroked it up and down while holding one of her cheeks apart. He smiled victoriously, finding her slick entrance, and guided his one-eyed snake towards it.

"Just like I thought, nigga, you ain't shit. Goo ain't been dead forty-eight hours and yo trifling ass already trying to run up in his bitch," Paperchase thought he heard Scorpion say.

He looked around wide-eyed, trying to see what area of the house his brother was spying on him from, but he didn't see him.

On gang, a nigga tripping hard than a muthafucka! I gotta lay off the Xannies for real, for real, Paperchase thought before grabbing his dick again to enter Brielle.

"I just know the homie Goo looking down from the heavens disgusted and disappointed with yo disloyal ass," he heard Scorpion's voice again. Spooked, he put his dick back in his jeans and zipped them up. He grabbed his hoodie and shirt, slipping them over his head and sticking his right hand through the sleeve first.

"What's the matter, Paperchase?" Brielle turned around to him, fixing her bathrobe on her luscious body and tied it tighter around her waist.

"I—I gotta go. I'll—I'll get up witchu later to see if you need anything," Paperchase told her as he tucked his gun and headed for the front door.

"Well, I need some dick." Brielle frowned as she followed him towards the door.

"You got plenty of gwop on the table, ma. Hit one of them gigolo niggaz hands; they'll get you right," Paperchase said over his shoulder as he hurried down the front porch steps.

"Nigga, I don't pay for dick!" Brielle hollered out to him while standing in the front doorway. "Fuck! I almost had that

nigga, man! Shit!" she slammed the door shut and went about the task of bagging the piles of money separately.

Paperchase wasn't anyone's fool. He knew the angle Brielle was trying to work. She would eventually blow through that bag he just dropped on her, and with Goo out of the picture, she'd need someone else to maintain the lifestyle she'd grown accustomed to. That's where Paperchase came in. If shorty knew one thing about him, it was that he was one hustling ass nigga. If there was a dollar to be made, he definitely was going to get it.

Brielle was going to be the one to wind up looking like a buffoon in the end. Paperchase would have dicked her down, but he sure as hell wasn't going to wife her up. Shit, he couldn't see how Goo pumped her ass with twins knowing how she got down. Little mama was a known slide throughout all five boroughs, so making her his baby mama was a no, no. Then again, who was he to talk? He'd almost ran up in her raw a few minutes ago and risked having a baby by her.

Yo, son, you be wildin'. You've gotta learn to chill. You almost got us caught up again with these broads. We already done fucked bro over, Paperchase thought as he stole a glance down at his lap. He focused his attention back on the road, pulled out his cellphone, and hit up Jabari.

"What up, my nig?" Jabari asked, picking up on the second ring.

"Shit. Where you at, though? I needa holla at you ASAP," Paperchase replied.

"Word? What's goodie, niggaz got problems?"

"Nah, chill, cowboy, ain't shit like that. I just needa a word with you."

"Oh, well, I'm at the crib. You can slide through."

"Aiight bet. Gimme, like, fifteen minutes."

"Bet."

Paperchase disconnected the call and laid his cellphone down on the console. He turned the volume up on Pooh Shiesty's latest and picked up the speed in his car.

155

***

Jabari took his gun case down from the top shelf of the closet and laid it down on the bed. He unlocked it, lifted its lid, and a P89 Ruger was lying on a bed of soft cushioning before him. Two fully loaded magazines and a silencer were on opposing sides of it. Jabari loaded the gun, cocked it, and screwed the silencer onto its barrel. He slipped his arms inside the sleeves of his bomber jacket with the fury around its hood and stuck the P89 in its inside pocket. He stepped before the mirror over the dresser and practiced drawing that bitch. He found his action a little too slow.

"This shit not gon' work, son. Wait a minute; maybe I can pop him through my jacket's pocket," Jabari thought aloud. He turned to the side, grabbed hold of his gun while it was still inside his jacket's pocket, and pointed it at his reflection in the mirror.

Yeah, that will work, Jabari thought. He fixed his jacket on him and walked out of his bedroom. He flipped off the light switch and headed for the front door.

Chapter 24

Paperchase sat in his car waiting for Jabari and drumming his fingers on the steering wheel. His head was on a swivel taking in his surroundings. He had to be on point because his enemies would love to get the recognition that came with assassinating him. He adjusted his rearview mirror and saw Jabari jogging in his direction. He knocked on the passenger window, Paperchase popped the locks, and he jumped in the front seat.

"What up, fool?" Jabari extended his hand.

"What up?" Paperchase shook up with him. "I've been fucking that bitch Liv behind bro back."

"What the fuck? Son, I just hopped in this bitch, and you drop that shit on me? Goddamn, you didn't even ease into it, just bam, 'Yo, I've been fucking that bitch Liv behind bro back.'"

"You know I've never been the one for small talk. I like to put shit out there and see how a nigga takes it first. You feel me?" Paperchase asked. He plucked a half-smoked blunt from the ashtray and lit it up. He took a couple of pulls from it and passed it to Jabari.

Bloooood, if the big homie found out this nigga was laying the pipe to his bitch, he'd skin his black ass alive, Jabari thought, shaking his head. *I got the nigga line. I should tell his ass and let him do my dirty work for me. But there's no telling how long it would take for him to get a steppa to get the job done.*

"Aye, aye, you listening to me? A nigga gotta get this shit off his chest, bro," Paperchase said. He snapped his fingers before Jabari's eyes, and he zapped back to the present. He'd gotten so wrapped up in his thoughts he couldn't hear him talking.

"My bad, bro. Nigga went somewhere else." Jabari hit the blunt again.

"I see. Anyway, Blood, the shit just happened," Paperchase went on. "I slid out to her crib one night to drop bruh's cut off so she could put it away for him. She invited me in for a drink, we got real saucy, and one thing led to the next. Ever since then, I

haven't been able to keep my dick to myself," he took the blunt from Jabari. "That ain't all either, my nigga."

Paperchase gave Jabari the rundown on what happened during the mission Scorpion had sent him and Goo on. He even told him about how he almost fucked one of Goo's baby mamas too. Although he felt like shit revealing these embarrassing ass details, he and Jabari went way back. If there was anyone he trusted with his deepest darkest secrets, it was most definitely him.

"So that's why you dropped by to holla at me? You needed yo therapist and shit." Jabari smirked. "I should start making you hit my hand for these sessions."

Paperchase laughed. "You're a real comedian, bro. You should do standup."

"That's entirely too slow for yo boy. I like that fast money," Jabari replied. "Why you think I fell in love with these streets?"

"Sho you right. Look, I got a lil' something, something for you," Paperchase said, switching hands with the blunt and reaching into the backseat.

Seeing he wasn't paying him any mind, Jabari gripped his gun from inside his jacket and pointed it at him. His finger slowly embraced its trigger. He was about to send his soul soaring towards the heavenly skies, but he abruptly turned around, startling him. Paperchase looked at him suspiciously while holding the small shopping bag. "What the fuck is the matter with you?"

"Shit, nigga, it's cold in here. Fuck you wanted to give me?"

Paperchase sat the small shopping bag into his lap. Smoking the blunt, he watched him closely as he removed the graphic t-shirt inside of the shopping bag. A smile spread across his lips as he pulled out two five-thousand-dollar stacks. "Yo, son, what you want me to do with this?" He looked at him.

"Whatever you want. It's not mine; it's yours," Paperchase assured him. "That's half the profit I got for fencing that D.A. nigga's jewels, Dunn. Fifty geez. It's only right that I break bread with my main man, you know how we do."

"That's love, fool." Jabari slapped hands and shook up with him.

"Love, my nigga." Paperchase pulled him in and patted his back.

Just when I was about to rock Slime to sleep, he goes and pulls a stunt like this. Nigga had always looked out for the kid, even when we were knee-high to a grasshopper. The more I think about it; I can't do it. I can't stank Blood. He is my brother. Shit, I love this nigga to death.

All the ups and downs Jabari and Paperchase had been through played in his mind's eye. He felt overwhelmed with guilt and sadness, realizing he'd eventually have to blow his best friend off the map. He tried to convince himself that it was a necessary evil because, with his death, the game would be wide opened for him. He'd be a fool to turn down the wealth and power he'd receive, aligning himself with Sanka. An offer like his only came around once in a lifetime, if at all, so it was best to capitalize off of it when the opportunity presented itself.

"Aye, bruh, I'ma take it in the house. I'ma get up with you tomorrow, though." Jabari took the small shopping bag into his other hand. He was about to hop out of the car, but Paperchase called him back.

"I'ma pull up in front of yo crib, my nigga. Never know, the opps could be lurking," Paperchase told him.

"You're right about that," Jabari replied settling down in his seat.

Paperchase cranked up his SRT, busted a U-turn in the middle of the street, and drove up alongside the curb of his right-hand man's house. They shook up again, and Jabari hopped out. Paperchase watched him enter his yard and lower the latch on the gate behind him. He opened the front door of his house and threw their hood up at him. Paperchase threw it back up at him. Once he went inside the house and slammed the door shut, he drove off with tears manifesting in his eyes. As soon as the wetness slid down his cheeks, he wiped it away.

He reached in the small pouch attached to the back of the front passenger seat and pulled out his gun. Earlier, when he'd reached in the backseat for the shopping bag, he was actually going for the

piece. He had every intention of blowing Jabari's brain on the dashboard, but he changed his mind at the last second.

"I couldn't do it. I couldn't bring myself to noodle him." Paperchase shook his head and tucked his banga between the seat and console. "That's been my dog since the sandbox. How the fuck am I gon' bring myself drill him?"

Hearing his cellphone ringing, Paperchase looked at its screen to see who was hitting him up. He wasn't going to answer it, but the man calling him wasn't someone you ignored. With that in mind, Paperchase picked up the call.

"What's up?" Paperchase asked the caller as he busted a right turn.

"I think we both know the answer to that," the caller said. "Have you completed your assignment yet?"

"No. I haven't but—"

The caller disconnected the call, leaving Paperchase's mind wandering. He tried dialing the caller back, but he didn't answer.

"Fuck," Paperchase said. He banged his fist on the steering wheel and thought back to the day he'd gotten himself in this position. It wasn't long ago.

One minute he was talking to Sanka, and the next, a black pillowcase was being pulled over his head, and he felt what was equivalent to a bee sting to the side of his neck. Sometime later, he came to inside of a palace fit for Nigerian royalty. The place was plush with unique, colorful furniture and portraits of prominent African figures hanging on the walls. Sanka was sitting before him on a golden throne, with a lion on both sides of him. He was dressed in the finest of midnight blue silk pajamas. His top was open to show his chiseled chest and six-pack abs. He was grinning and sipping something from a golden chalice decorated with black, red, and green diamonds. Paperchase tried to get up from his chair, and his knees buckled. He almost fell, but the two beautiful black Barbie Dolls, who he hadn't noticed at first, standing on both sides of him, caught him and helped him sit back down. He was lightheaded and felt weak, but he was given a drink in a smaller chalice similar to Sanka's. Shortly, he was back to his normal self,

and Sanka was asking him about his parents and their lineage. He took an interest in the fact that his old man was a full-blooded Nigerian but moved the conversation along.

"Paperchase, what I have in store for you is guaranteed to make you a very rich man. All I ask is for is your complete cooperation. You do what I say and how I say it, no questions asked. You follow my directives and know that if ever you step outside of them that there will be consequences with no mercy. Do you understand that?"

"Yeah, I got you."

Paperchase got the feeling Sanka had given this speech millions of times. He wasn't even listening to him until he guaranteed to make him rich. After that, he was making note of everything he was being told and asked of him. Sanka wanted him to flood the city with this new dope. It was said to be ten times more addictive than regular heroin, and once you got hooked on it, there wasn't any way you could get off it. He called it Rebirth. Paperchase couldn't wait to get his hands on this new product. He'd already come up with some ideas on how to market it. This proposition seemed too good to be true. He knew there had to be a catch to it because no one was just going to hand you something, especially if your ass was black.

"...You see, with every new position comes a great sacrifice. Your position is no different. We demand three sacrifices. We choose, of course, all three, but the first will be very simple."

"I'm with whatever that's gon' put me in the position of power. The fact I'm sitting here is proof enough you done your homework on me, so you know catching a body ain't nothing new to me. So, who's first on the hit list?" Paperchase smiled and rubbed his hands together greedily. He was thinking about all the dough he was going to make once Sanka put him on.

Sanka found amusement in how anxious Paperchase was to get the ball rolling on their promising business venture. He was positive that shit was going to change once he dropped the name of the first nigga on the list.

"Your man Jabari." Sanka grinned devilishly and drank from his chalice. The palace was impregnated with an uncomfortable silence.

A surprised expression came across Paperchase face, and he slumped in his chair. "Aye, Sanka, homie you mentioned is like my brother. Slime is fam. I couldn't possibly take him off his feet. I'm willing to drill anyone else, though. I mean, anybody. Shiiiit, I'll even grease Jake. They ain't shit but Klansmen with badges anyway."

Sanka really wanted Jabari hit now that he'd seen Paperchase's reaction. He wanted to see exactly how far he was willing to go to obtain the financial freedom he'd placed on the table before him.

"Jabari shall be the first sacrifice." Sanka replied sternly as he caressed the head of the lion on his left. He watched as Paperchase thought things over and massaged his chin. If he didn't agree to assassinate Jabari, he would give his lions word to ravage him.

"Aiight, fuck it. If this is what I gotta do to ascend to the next level in this game, then I'm with it."

"Good. You have three months."

Paperchase had been on a time clock ever since then. He knew he'd have to deliver on his end of the deal, or he'd likely become Sanka's lions next meal.

Chapter 25

It was two o'clock in the afternoon, and Jabari was still asleep from a night of partying like a rock star. He had crust in his eyes and dried drool at the corner of his mouth. His nostrils flared as he snored, and his lips trembled. The sound of humming and chirping disturbed his sleep. He scrunched his face and peeled his eyes open, taking in his surroundings with blurred vision. Once his sight came into focus, he saw a Ruby-throated Hummingbird flying around outside of his bedroom window. Turning over on his back, he yawned and stretched his arms above his head. He sat up in bed, rubbing his eyes and scratching his nuts, when he was surprised by the sight at the foot of his bed.

"Blood, what the fuck?" Jabari's eyes bucked. He back peddled in bed until he bumped up against the headboard, and then he went to grab his gun from underneath his pillow. He came up empty-handed, so he smacked the pillow aside. The gun wasn't there.

"Are you looking for this?" one of the two Nigerians at the end of his bed asked, pointing the gun he was looking for at him. He and his comrade were dressed in Filas and green Dashiki pants suits. They wore matching Coronavirus masks over their nose and mouth. The look in their eyes would have intimidated a lesser man, but Jabari was a gangsta.

"Y—yeah," Jabari replied with his hands up. Right then, there were two things posing a threat to his life: the gun homeboy had aimed at his chest and that big ass lion his comrade was holding the leash of.

The Nigerian popped the clip out the bottom of the gun and ejected the copper bullet. He caught the bullet in mid-air, tossed the gun back to Jabari, and threw the bullet over his shoulder.

"Yo, can y'all put that muthafucka in the bathroom or something? He's making me nervous," he referred to the lion who was just sitting there staring at him.

"Don't worry, he and his brother ate an entire buffalo half an hour ago, so he shouldn't be hungry for a while," the Nigerian

holding the lion's leash assured him as he stroked his fine golden coat of hair.

"Shouldn't be?" Jabari looked at him sideways. "Look, man, I don't know how y'all got in my spot, but what the fuck do y'all want?"

"You came to an agreement with Sanka, did you not?" the Nigerian that tossed him the gun asked.

"Yeah. Bruh, he and I have an understanding."

"As you know, he has been trying to contact you to get an update, but you have deliberately ignored his calls."

"What? Dog, I haven't ignored shit. I've been…"

Jabari was cut short when the Nigerian he was talking to pulled out a cellphone. He showed him footage of him in Off The Wall sitting in the VIP section, looking at the call he'd gotten from Sanka and then putting his cellular away. Jabari tried to think of a lie, but he couldn't formulate one on the spot, so he decided to let what the Nigerian said rock.

"You should know that Sanka takes it as a personal insult when someone ignores him. It makes him very, very angry. And let me assure you, *son*," he said with an accent close to Jabari's. "You do not want to see the king angry." Jabari nodded his understanding. "If you'd like to pull out of the deal, then I suggest you say so now. With Sanka, time is money, and he doesn't have any to waste."

"Nah. Tell big homie I'm still with the shits. I'ma get what he needs done soon. I'm talking real soon. I know I'm on the clock, and I'ma make it happen," Jabari assured him.

"Good. This here is for you." The Nigerian pulled out a Ziploc bag loaded with packets of dope and tossed it to Jabari. He caught the bag, held it up, and examined its contents. He didn't bother asking what he had in his possession because he already knew what it was—Rebirth. "Sanka thinks it will be best that you see what the Rebirth can do. So, he wants you to bless the streets with some of it and observe the reaction you get from it. Maybe once you get a taste of the money to be made, it will put a little pep in your step to getting things done."

King of the Trenches

The Nigerians gave a curtsey nod to Jabari before leaving his bedroom and then his house. Jabari hopped out of bed, ran into his living room, and peered out of the blinds. It fucked him up seeing the Nigerians walking that big ass lion out of his yard like it was a pit-bull. A couple of neighborhood kids ran up on the wild animal, asking could they pet it. The Nigerians agreed, and the kids did as they pleased.

Jabari made sure his front door was locked. He took care of his hygiene, made a few calls, and then got dressed for the day. The last thing he did was reload the gun the Nigerian had tossed back to him and put one in its head. He tucked his piece in the small of his back, grabbed his car keys, his cellular, and dashed to the front door.

***

Ramone leaned back, yawning and stretching his arms above his head. He could hear his bones cracking and popping as they reset themselves. He staggered out of his bedroom, rubbing his stomach and his eye. A fog was still covering his brain from his being intoxicated the night before, so he was a little off-balance. He looked at the clock on the living room wall, and it was two-thirty in the evening. Well past the breakfast hour. Still, he'd promised himself he was going to cook breakfast for his mother, and nothing short of death was going to stop him from following through with his plans.

Ramone stopped at his mother's bedroom door, yawning and scratching his stomach. "Ma, I know it's late in the day, but fuck it. I'ma whip us up a nice breakfast. How does pancakes, eggs sunny side up, maple sausages, hash, grits, and orange juice sound?" he listened for her reply, but he didn't get it. He took a deep breath and leaned closer to the door.

"Come on now, ma, I know you're not still mad. I did what I did for the good of both of us. Hopefully, once you get better, you'll realize that." Again, he listened for her response, but it never came. He frowned, figuring something was up. He recovered the keys for his mother's bedroom door and unlocked all of its

locks. He was shocked to see Martha was gone! The window was open, and the curtains were ruffling from the wind blowing.

Ramone kneeled down to the shackle and picked it up. It was unlocked, so he figured his mother had managed to pick it somehow. He walked over to the window, and a homemade rope was hanging out of it. It was made out of Martha's clothes, underwear, sheets, blankets, and whatever else she could find to lengthen it. He looked down out of the window, and the home-made rope nearly reached the ground.

Never underestimate the determination of a dope fiend!

***

Ramone ran out of his bedroom and slipped on what he'd worn to the strip club. He hurried out of his unit, stuffing his barefeet inside of his Timbs. He slammed the door behind him, locked it, and hauled ass down the hallway. The elevator was taking too long, so he took the staircase. He spilled out of the glass doors of the red-bricked building and crashed to the asphalt. The bright, blazing sun shone on his face as he scrambled back upon his boots.

Ramone ran past kids playing Hide & Seek, little girls playing Double Dutch, resident knuckleheads smoking weed, and watching a freestyle rap cipher. He ran over to the side of the building that the homemade rope was hanging down. He looked up the tenement narrowing his eyes from the intense rays of the sun. Although the homemade rope was long, it was still quite a long drop to the ground. Ramone made a 360-degree turn looking for Martha, but she wasn't anywhere in sight. He ran around to the knuckleheads and the kids, asking if they'd seen his mother, whom they all knew. They all either shook their head or claimed to have not seen her.

Honk, honk, honk!

Ramone turned around from the kids he was questioning and saw Jabari's Charger parked in the red zone alongside the curb. He was hanging out of his window, waving him over to his ride. Ramone frowned, wondering why he'd just popped up at his house

without hitting him up first. He reasoned shit must have been serious if he made a home visit, so he jogged across the courtyard to his whip. Once he had reached his car, he looked down through the passenger side window at him.

"What up, son? Whatever's got you popping up in The Bricks and shit unannounced must be mad serious," Ramone said. He reached through the window and shook up with him.

"Straight up. Yo, take this ride with me, King. I needa kick it to you," Jabari replied.

Ramone looked to his left and right like he was searching for something or someone before focusing back on Jabari. "You want me to take a ride witchu right now?" he asked like he had something else of importance to do, which he did.

"Yeah, you got some shit up or something? Gotta lil' slide up in yo' spot, bro?" Jabari cracked a one-sided grin at him.

"Nah, nah, nah, nothing like that—it's just—it's just."

"It's just what, my G? Spit that shit out!" Jabari spoke with seriousness now. "You're my right hand, so if you've got a problem, then *we* gotta problem."

Ramone nodded his understanding. On the one hand, he wanted to scour the streets looking for his mother. But on the other hand, he wanted to see what was shaking with Jabari because it could put him in a better position than he was now.

Fuck it! I'll see what's up with Maduke's after I see what bruh wants. Nine times outta ten, she's somewhere shooting up, so I'll have him take me around to some of the dope spots I know, Ramone thought.

"Something is up, but it can wait," Ramone told him as he hopped into the car and slammed the door shut. Jabari looked at his side-view mirror before pulling out into traffic and driving away. "So, what's up? What you wanted to talk to me about?"

"The next nigga we've gotta knock over on our rise to power," Jabari told him without taking his eyes off the road.

"Who is that?" Ramone asked curiously.

"Paperchase," Jabari said nonchalantly. He glanced at him through the corner of his eye to see his reaction.

"Paperchase? But I thought that was yo mans?" Ramone frowned.

"Blood is in my way. No. Fuck that! He's in *our* way," Jabari said with a scowl. "Look, my nigga, I fucks with you the long way. We from the same borough, and I see myself in you. But if you not willing to do what it takes to put us in position, I'll let you out right here and find myself another soldier to get busy—one that carries out orders without question."

Jabari pulled over on the side of the road and popped the locks. He wore a dead serious expression on his face as he looked over at Ramone. He could tell by the look on his face he was thinking about what he was being asked to do. The young nigga knew Paperchase, and he had love for him. So, he found it difficult to carry out his execution for the betterment of his situation. But then again, if taking him out would appease Jabari and progress their movement, he was on board. Besides, he and Jabari were far closer than he and Paperchase were. His loyalty belonged to Jabari without a doubt.

"Aiight, dog, I'm with it," Ramone told him.

Jabari pressed the button that automatically locked the doors and pulled back off into New York City traffic. He held the steering wheel with one hand as he chopped it up with Ramone.

"Last time I hollered at bro, he was linking up with that bitch Olivia to drop off some loot for the big homie. I know where they normally meet up to make that transaction," Jabari told him. Ramone nodded as he half-listened to Jabari. He was staring at the streets they were whipping past, hoping he'd see his mother. "

Yo, son," Jabari nudged Ramone, and he looked at him. "Are you listening to me?"

"Yeah, I'm listening. You know where Paperchase and Olivia are meeting up for him to drop her off a bag for his bro."

"Right. So, all you gotta do is slip up in there, do what you do and slide out."

Ramone nodded his understanding. "Sounds easy enough. Is shorty going along for the ride too?"

"That all depends on you, my nigga. Either nod that half-breed bitch or don't. I really don't give a fuck, nah mean?" Ramone nodded.

"Check this out, Boobie and that nigga Durty gon' hold you down. We're rolling to the spot now, so you can hop in their ride with them."

"You want me to go on the mission wearing this?" Ramone asked with a frown, looking down at his attire.

"Not at all, I gotta nice lil' get up for you to wear. Niggaz won't even know who you are. Trust me," Jabari told him, turning the volume up on CJ's *Whoopty*. He then sped up the block, leaving debris in his wake.

Ghost & Tranay Adams

Chapter 26

Boobie and Durty were posted up outside of a black-on-black Chevrolet Tahoe kicking the shit while waiting for Jabari. They were inside of the exact same warehouse they'd trained Ramone how to kill with paintball guns. The sound of gravel being crushed drew their attention to the opposite entrance of the warehouse, where they saw a Benz driving up. The bright headlights of the vehicle made them narrow their eyes and reach for their waistbands. They relaxed once the headlights turned off, and they could see Jabari and Ramone sitting up front. The men swapped pleasantries and shook up. Durty opened the backdoor of the Tahoe and grabbed a shopping bag from Party City. He passed the shopping bag to Ramone, who then held it open and peered inside of it. The bag's contents were a blonde wig, black sunglasses, a hoodie, and makeup to make his hue resemble that of a Caucasian.

"Fuck is this shit?" Ramone asked Jabari.

"Your get up," Jabari told him. "Now hurry up and get dressed so y'all can handle that, King."

"Don't worry. I got it handled," Ramone replied as he stripped down to his wife-beater and boxer briefs. He sprayed on the Caucasian cosmetic makeup, pulled the blonde wig over his short dreadlocks, slipped on his black sunglasses, and put on the hoodie. Once he threw the hood over his head, he asked the guys how he looked and if they could tell it was him underneath the disguise.

"Nah, bruh, you can't tell it's you," Durty said as he circled Ramone thinking and massaging his chin.

"Yeah, son, I'm with Durty. We can't tell it's you wearing that disguise," Boobie gave him his opinion. "You just look like some cracka's son, B." He and the rest of the homies laughed at the thought.

"Y'all niggaz wildin', yo." Ramone laughed and shook his head. He stuffed the clothes he'd had on previously inside of the shopping bag and handed it to Jabari.

"Y'all niggaz go ahead before that nigga's gone," Jabari told Boobie and Durty. They shook up with him and walked back

towards the Tahoe. Ramone followed closely behind them but turned back around when he was called back.

Ramone jogged back over to Jabari. "What's the deal?"

"Dig this. I know you fuck with bruh, so it's probably gon' fuck witchu mentally having to take him out and all," Jabari told him. "With that said, I brought along a lil' something for you to get yo mind right before you do yo thang." He pulled out a baggie of cocaine from his bomber jacket and passed it to him. Ramone looked at it and put it in his pocket.

"Make me proud, King." Jabari shook up with Ramone and patted him on the back. He watched him hop into the Tahoe with Boobie and Durty. Once they were gone, Jabari hopped into his whip and vanished from the warehouse.

***

Now that Jabari had sent Ramone away on his mission, it was time he tied up a loose end. His mind switched to the heated discussion between him and Jayshawn. He had mad love for him and Ramone and sort of looked at them like extended family, but all that was about to change. Jayshawn had him fucked up on so many levels for thinking he could talk to a nigga of his caliber the way he had. He was known as a big stepper throughout Brooklyn. His opps feared and respected him. He'd locked ass with some of the most reputable killaz to have ever touched a New York City block. So, he'd be damned if he let some dusty, bum-ass nigga talk to him like he didn't dance with wolves and bust his gun.

Jabari was a cold-blooded hitta, and he felt like Jayshawn had forgotten about that. That was okay, though, because he was on his way to give his ass a reminder.

Jabari drove his Dodge Charger up his driveway and inside of his garage. As the garage door was closing behind him, he was hopping out of the car and slamming the door shut. He stripped down to his wife-beater and boxer briefs and stepped into a leather black and red motorcycle suit. He laced his boots, put on his gloves, and drew a large plastic knife he'd forged for this very mission from its hiding place. Jabari approached the beige bust of

a rubber mannequin standing up against the wall. He took a professional stance with his knife at his side and swiftly stabbed the left side of its torso four times. The blade went through the dummy quite easily, so he knew he wouldn't have any trouble putting it through Jayshawn.

Jabari snatched off one of his gloves and pressed his thumb against the tip of the plastic knife. Blood oozed into the form of a dot on his thumb. Sucking his thumb, he smiled wickedly and nodded with the satisfaction of his fine-crafted weapon. He pulled his glove back over his hand and flexed his fingers inside of it. He unzipped his motorcycle suit and sheathed his plastic knife inside of it. He pocketed a white Coronavirus mask, pulled his motorcycle helmet over his head, and climbed onto his Ducati SuperSport. Kicking up its kickstand, he turned on his bike and revved it up. The motorcycle whined loud and annoyingly.

Jabari pressed the button on the wall that activated the garage door. As soon as the door lifted up, he revved up his Ducati again and zipped down the driveway. He made a right onto the paved residential street and zipped up the boulevard. He Popped-A-Wheelie halfway down the road, came down and zipped up the block faster. A moment later, the red taillight of his bike disappeared into the darkness like an apparition.

Jabari parked his Ducati in a nearby alley. He camouflaged it underneath cardboard, old newspapers, black garbage bags, and a few other items littering the path. Still in his helmet, he walked across the street and made his way onto hospital grounds. The security guard was asleep at the front desk with his cap pulled low over his brows, so he didn't prove a problem getting by.

Jabari was walking down the elevator lobby when he noticed one of the hospital's janitors. He was a fifty-ish white man wearing a cap, a Coronavirus mask, and Dickie jumpsuit. He was pushing his cleaning cart onto an elevator car that had just arrived. Jabari looked at the up and down buttons on the panel. The up button was lit, so he knew he was going up. The elevator's doors were almost closed until he stuck his gloved hand between them.

They reopened, and he stepped inside. He exchanged nods with the janitor and pressed the number to the floor he desired.

Jabari posted up at the back of the elevator and opened his helmet's visor. He examined the janitor closely, figuring they wore the same size in clothing and shoes. Glancing at the numbers they'd selected on the panel, he noticed they had a few stops left before they reached the floor he'd personally selected. With that in mind, he made his move swiftly. He slipped up behind the older man and applied the Sleeper Hold to him. The man gritted and struggled to break the hold.

"Shhhhhhh. Relax, Pops. You look like you could use a nap," Jabari told him. Seconds later, his movements slowed, and he'd fallen asleep, snoring. Jabari laid him down inside of the elevator and pressed the emergency stop button. He removed his helmet, unzipped his leather suit, and began getting dressed in his victim's uniform.

***

The elevators doors opened. Jabari rolled out the cleaning cart wearing his cap pulled low and the Coronavirus mask. He left the janitor slumped against the elevator wall wearing his helmet and motorcycle suit. Jabari was halfway down the hallway to Jayshawn's room by the time the elevator's doors closed. The window of opportunity was closing fast. He knew it was only a matter of time before the janitor was discovered inside of the elevator, and the staff came looking for answers. He wanted to make Jayshawn's death bloody and extremely painful, but time wouldn't permit it. He'd have to alternate and settle for quick and clean.

Jabari stopped his cleaning cart at Jayshawn's hospital door. He looked up and down the hallway. The few staff that was around weren't paying any attention to him. They were too busy talking among themselves and completing tasks. Jabari stole a look inside of the dark room. Jayshawn was lying in bed asleep with the glow of the television's screen dancing across his face.

Jabari pulled his plastic knife from inside his Dickie jumpsuit, gripping it like Michael Myers and creeping upon Jayshawn's bedside.

This is going to be like taking candy from a baby.

***

The Chevrolet Tahoe sat idling in the alley three houses down from Olivia's crib. M.O.P's *Ante up* was pumping so loudly from its speakers the entire truck was vibrating. The SUV was filled with smoke as Boobie and Durty were passing a blunt of Jamaica's finest between them while Ramone tooted coke up his nose in the backseat. Ramone snorted up the last of the cocaine from his fist and threw his head back. "Wooooo!" he shouted like Ric Flair, looking around and blinking his teary eyes. He then snorted like a warthog, dug in his nose, and then pulled on it.

Boobie passed the blunt to Durty. He adjusted the rearview mirror and looked up into it. He was so startled by Ramone's demonic appearance that he clutched his gun tighter.

"Blood, what the fucks up witchu?" Durty asked off of his reaction. Boobie threw his head toward the backseat. Durty looked over his shoulder and was taken aback by Ramone's terrifying appearance as well. The young nigga looked like a crazed psychopath. "Yo, you good, son?"

"Yeah, yeah, I'm good, Dunn. I'm just ready to drill some shit, ya heard?" Ramone slipped on his black sunglasses, threw his hood over his head, and whipped out his black leather gloves. "Yo, crank that shit up; I'm getting in my zone."

Ramone pulled the black leather gloves over his hands as he spat the lyrics to the song. The mixture of cocaine and crunked-up music had him amped up. He cocked the slide on his gun, putting a hollow tip bullet in its chamber. It was now a deadly weapon!

Ramone jumped out of the truck, tucked his piece in his waistband, and made his way towards Olivia's crib with murder on his mind.

Chapter 27

Paperchase had to link up with Olivia this day to drop off Scorpion's cut from the moves he'd been making in the streets. He was driving up her block when he saw her pass something concealed in a towel to someone in a white BMW X6 with red-tinted windows. He didn't have a clue as to who the driver was, but he could make out their silhouette through the red-tinted windows of their whip. It was most definitely a woman. A tall one at that. He couldn't tell for sure, but he thought she'd glanced at him in passing.

Paperchase pulled his SRT into Olivia's driveway, killed the engine, and hopped out. She stood on her front porch with her hands folded across her breasts, waiting for him. He popped his trunk open and grabbed a Gucci knapsack from out of it. He slung one of its straps over his shoulder, glanced at his Rollie, and jogged up the short steps that led to the porch.

"Yo, who was shorty that was just over here?" Paperchase asked out of curiosity.

"Why? You jealous?" Olivia grinned. She then pulled him so close to her he could smell the minty toothpaste she'd used to brush her teeth. "If you are, then don't be, Pa 'cause you're the only nigga Fat Ma gets wet for," she whispered into his ear while cuffing the bulge in his jeans.

"Relax. I already told you what it is from now on between us." Paperchase gently pushed her back. "Now, let's go inside, get this money counted up so you can make sure it gets to bro's offshore account." He brushed past her, heading inside of the house and leaving her on the front porch, looking stupid as fuck. She grinned, licked her top row of teeth, and spun on her heels. She marched inside of the house, shut the door behind her, and locked it.

Paperchase dumped the contents of the Gucci knapsack onto the kitchen table. He pulled out a chair, sat down, and began removing the rubber bands from around the stacks of dead presidents. Olivia rifled through the cupboards and cabinets inside of the kitchen for the money counter. A look of frustration was on

her face having trouble finding it, and she was bitching about it under her breath.

"Dónde diablos está esa maldita máquina? Sé que lo puse aquí en alguna parte (Where the fuck is that goddamn machine? I know I put it in here somewhere)," Olivia complained. Suddenly, she stopped rifling through the cabinets and a smile spread across her face. "There you are. I knew I put you somewhere in here." She grabbed the money counter from where it was hidden behind the pots and pans, set it down on the kitchen table, and pulled up a chair.

Paperchase pulled out a half-ounce bag of Purple Kush and began breaking it down on the kitchen table. He knew exactly how much bread he was kicking up to Scorpion, having counted it three times. But every time he made a drop-off to Olivia for her to deposit, he made her count it again in front of him so there wouldn't be any misunderstanding. Although he was putting the pipe to Olivia and he had feelings for her, he wasn't going to let his emotions cloud his judgment. Paperchase knew as well as anyone else that chances were that if the opposite sex or money was involved, circumstances and people changed. He didn't raise a fuss about it. That was just how it was.

Paperchase had smoked a little more than half of his blunt by the time Olivia had finished counting up the money and putting rubber bands back around it. He watched carefully as she reloaded the Gucci knapsack with blue cheese, drew the strings, closed its flap, and then slung its strap over her shoulder. She made her way inside of her bedroom to hide the knapsack until she went to holler at Scorpion's banker tomorrow.

As soon as Olivia was out of his sight, Paperchase mashed out what was left of his blunt and placed it behind his ear. He slipped on his jacket and stashed what was left of the Kush inside of his jacket's pocket. He then snatched up his car keys and walked to the front door. He'd just unlocked the door and pulled it open when Olivia came out of nowhere and pushed it shut.

"And just where do you think you're going, mister?" Olivia asked, grabbing the collar of his jacket and walking him back-

wards. The only thing she had on now was her bra and panties. She'd been planning to make her move on Paperchase as soon as they were done conducting business.

"I've got business to take care of, Liv. I don't have time to play with yo ass. So, move outta my way," Paperchase said irritated, shoving her out of his way. He reached for the doorknob, but she grabbed his hand and swung his arm around her waist. She grabbed his other hand and swung it around as well.

She licked his neck over his throat and started sucking the soft flesh below his chin. In the midst of doing this, she slid his strong masculine hands down the small of her back and forcibly made him cuff her buttocks. She licked his lips and sucked on his bottom one, gently pulling on it. She slipped her tongue inside of his mouth. They closed their eyes and started kissing. The sound of their saliva moving inside of their mouths and their moaning filled the living room. Paperchase gripped both of her globes, and the meat of them seeped between his fingers. He began rubbing all over her ass and then groping them like they were a pair of perky titties. Before he knew it, his dick was as hard as a baseball bat, and he was ready to hit something.

Paperchase tilted his head back and closed his eyes, moaning loudly. Olivia bit and sucked on his neck as she helped him out of his clothes. She'd gotten him down to his wife-beater when he started to realize what was happening.

"Stop, stop, stop!" Paperchase pushed her off him. He held up his hand to keep her where she was and used his other hand to wipe her red lipstick kisses off him.

Olivia caught herself before she could fall. She turned around and looked at Paperchase like he'd lost his goddamn mind. "Nigga, what the fuck is wrong with you?"

"Bitch, don't act brand new. I told you what was up when I came over here!" Paperchase spat angrily with his fists clenched at his sides. His face was balled up, and he was gritting his teeth. To her, he looked so cute when he was mad, especially now that he had the hickies she'd given him running up and down his neck.

"Oh, now it's foul, huh? It wasn't foul all the other times we got down," Olivia said as she rose to her pretty feet. She slowly walked toward him, unfastening her bra from the back. Her panties played hide and seek between her ample buttocks with every step she took.

"Well, it is now! And this shit is stopping today!" Paperchase barked and jabbed his finger at her.

"Nigga, you got me fucked up, ain't shit stopping!" Olivia barked back at him and smacked his hand down. She forced him up against the wall and grabbed his semi-erect dick. "You started this shit, and we're not done until I say we're done!" Her nose and lips grazed his as she spoke. Her demanding demeanor and feminine touch aroused him. She was driving him crazy, and he was finding it harder and harder to fight her off.

"Blood, this shit not right, we can't keep doing this to bro," Paperchase tried to reason with her, but she wasn't trying to hear him.

"What big brother doesn't know won't hurt him. Trust." Olivia sunk her teeth in the side of his neck and began sucking on it. She then took his hand and slid it inside of her panties. His fingers parted her rose petals, and he slipped one of his digits inside of her pink. She was sticky and oozing hot with her natural juices. The feel of her womanhood made him weak in the knees. He placed his head back against the wall, rolling his eyes and licking his lips. He felt her squeezing his piece while running her delicate hand up and down the length of it.

"You feel that, Papi? Huh? You feel that?"

"Y—yeah, Mami, I feel that shit," Paperchase replied in a hushed tone.

"It's so hot, juicy, and tight, just for you, Pa," Olivia swore, kissing up his neck and then sucking on the soft flesh below his chin. Clear pre-cum oozed out of his pee-hole and ran down his shaft. "Tell me you don't want none of this pussy. You look me in my eyes and tell me you don't want none of this pussy. If you can do that, I'll stop what I'm doing right now and leave," she told him between sucking on the soft flesh below his chin.

"I—I—I don't want none of this p—pussy," Paperchase managed to tell her with his eyes shut.

As soon as she pulled away from him, his eyes popped open, and he watched her pick her bra back up. She was about to put it back on until he pulled her into him. He lifted her up against the wall, and she wrapped her legs around his waist. Heavily breathing, they kissed hard and lustfully while he undid his jeans hastily. His jeans fell down around his thighs. He pulled her panties aside and shoved himself deep within her hidden valley. She threw her head back, fluttering her eyes and howling in a mixture of pain and bliss. He started fucking her savagely up against the wall. He knocked over the lamp on the nightstand in the midst of them getting busy. She slipped her hands underneath his shirt and clawed at his back. Her acrylic nails broke his skin, and blood seeped from the small wounds. His face balled up in pleasure and pain, and he started fucking her even harder. Her sexual screams bounced off the walls inside of the bedroom. And the banging up against the wall eventually caused a framed portrait to fall.

Chapter 28
Meanwhile

Errrn! The loud buzzer resonated through the federal facility. Metal door after metal door slid open and convicts emerged out of their cells onto the gallery. Among them was Scorpion. He made his way down the tier with a hardened expression on his face. He walked down the stairs and onto the landing. As he walked across the floor, he exchanged daps and what's ups? With the convicts within his organization and mean mug stares with those on the opposing side. He entered the visiting room, handing in his visitor's pass to the officer at the front desk. They swapped a few words before he continued on his way to the person that was visiting him. His head was on a swivel as he scanned every face in attendance. The wave of a pinkish hand caught his attention, and his eyes settled on the man he was looking forward to seeing that evening.

The gentleman waiting at the table for Scorpion went by the name Othman Cromwel. He was a fifty-five-year-old retired homicide detective who now ran his own private investigation firm. He was a heavy-set, clean-shaven man who sported a baldhead that shined like a buffed floor. He wore a sports coat over a polo shirt and stonewashed blue jeans. He rose to his feet and extended his hand towards Scorpion.

"Mr. Williams, how have you been?" Othman asked as they shook hands.

"I'm good," Scorpion replied, pulling his pants up at the knees and sitting down at the table.

"Great. You get a chance to check out the game last night? Boy, I tell ya, I had five grand riding on the Cavs, and those fuckers—" Othman was cut short when Scorpion abruptly raised his hand in the middle of him talking.

"Look, bruh, you and I have what you call an employer/ employee relationship, so all that conversing like old college buddies isn't necessary," Scorpion told him with a dead serious look on his

face. "I pay you good money for your services, and I'd like to know whether my baby girl is fucking around on me or not."

Something at the back of Scorpion's mind was nagging him about Olivia's loyalty to him. Although she'd sworn up and down that she hadn't been fucking around with anyone else, he couldn't shake the feeling that she wasn't being honest. He tried to tell himself he had a good girl and that she'd never do anything to break his heart, but he'd heard too many niggaz behind those walls crying themselves to sleep at night behind their woman getting dick down on the outside. He knew if he didn't find out for sure if his boo was creeping or not that his mind wouldn't allow him to rest. So, he decided to enlist Othman to get to the bottom of things and find out exactly what was going on.

Othman looked away, scratching the back of his baldhead. He then looked up at Scorpion, who wore a solemn expression as he waited for him to deliver his findings. The heavy-set man took a deep breath and leaned closer so only Scorpion could hear what he was about to say.

"Your sweet little angel isn't so innocent," Othman told him in a hushed tone.

The moment the words left his lips, Scorpion felt his heart drop and tumble across the floor. He suddenly felt dizzy and wanted to throw up. The G in him would never allow Othman to see how fucked up he was behind his wifey two-timing him, though.

"What exactly do you mean, bruh? Just come out and say it," Scorpion said with frustration. He was hoping he told him Olivia was calling, texting, or had gone out with some nigga on a date. He was sure they could salvage their relationship and work things out if that was the case. But there was no way they could live happily ever after if she was giving some other nigga what was his. That was something he most definitely couldn't live with. He'd have to off her and whatever clown she was laying up with.

"You know I came in here trying to break the news to you as gently as I possibly can 'cause I'm a nice guy, but if you want the raw uncut truth, I'll give it to ya, buddy," Othman said with a no-

nonsense attitude. "That fiancé of yours is getting it long, hard, and fast up the hoo-ha. I'm sorry to have to be the one to tell you, but that's just how it is." He took a deep breath and lay back in his chair.

Scorpion became teary-eyed clenching and unclenching his jaws while balling his fists. He was angry, hurt, and devastated— the news stung him like the venomous tail of a scorpion. To keep from breaking down and looking soft, Scorpion closed his eyes and ran his hands down his face. He then took a deep breath and scooted his chair up to the table. His heart ached like a mothafucka, but he had to get the question lingering in his head answered.

"Aiight, who is this nigga she's fucking around with?" Scorpion asked.

Othman sat up in his chair and leaned close enough so that only Scorpion could hear him. He told him the name of the person blowing his bitch's back out. His eyes bucked, and his mouth hung open in shock.

***

"Fuck me, brother, fuck me, fuck me! Oh God, yes! Yes!" Olivia hollered loud enough for the Lord and all of his angels in Heaven to hear her. Her eyes were squeezed shut, and her mouth was hanging open. She was high up on the wall with her arms and legs wrapped around Paperchase's waist. He sucked on her neck as he fucked her like a mad man. His back muscles flexed along with his buttocks. He was packing her ass out, running dick in and out of her, with his jeans in a pile around his ankles.

"This my pussy? Huh? This pussy belongs to me?" Paperchase asked with clenched jaws and possessed eyes. He was laying into her like he hated her guts.

"Yes, it's yours, lil' bro, it belongs to you! Only you!" Olivia hollered even louder, making Paperchase fuck her that much harder, grunting.

***

"You cocksucka, I'll kill you!" Scorpion bellowed as he lunged at Othman from the other side of the table. He collided with him, and they slammed into the floor with his hands wrapped around his neck. Straddling him, he squeezed his neck tighter and tighter, with spit hanging from the corner of his mouth. "I'll kill you! I'll fucking kill you, you mothafucka!"

"Ack, ack, ack, gag, gag, ack!" Othman turned beet red, and veins bulged over his forehead. His eyes widened, and he became teary. He tried his hardest to pry Scorpion's hands from around his neck, but his adrenaline added to his strength, made that impossible.

"You're lying. You're fucking lying!" Scorpion shouted with spit jumping off his lips and his eyes twinkling with tears.

All of the inmates and visitors in the room were looking at them in shock.

Othman looked like he was about to lose consciousness from lack of oxygen. He stopped trying to fight Scorpion off and lay there, letting him choke him.

"Die, die, you fucking asshole!" Scorpion hollered, and his spit clung to Othman's face.

***

The hot shower water began to fog the bathroom mirror while Paperchase studied his reflection. Hunched over the sink, he looked at himself like he didn't know who he was, having betrayed his brother by sleeping with Olivia. He'd tried a million times, but he couldn't stop fucking her. It was like he was a dope fiend, and she was the heroin—he was addicted to her.

"Damn, a nigga never thought he'd end up pussy whipped, but here I am." Paperchase shook his head sadly. He was ashamed. He could tell himself once again that this would be the last time he laid up with Olivia, but deep down inside, he knew he'd be lying to himself. He honestly didn't know what he was going to do if his brother was released from prison. "Fuck it. I'll just cross that bridge with bro once I come to it."

"Boy, who are you talking to?" Olivia asked as she stepped behind him naked and wrapped her arms around him. She placed the side of her face against his and looked at their reflections in the mirror. She started kissing on the side of his face and alongside his neck.

"No one—just thinking aloud." Paperchase flashed a weak smile and kissed her over his shoulder.

"Come on. I'ma need you to wash my back." Olivia smiled happily as she led him over to the glass enclosure by his hand.

***

Othman sat up on the floor with teary eyes coughing and rubbing his aching neck. A corrections officer was on either side of him, making sure he was okay.

"I'll be—I'll be fine," Othman nodded as he assured them.

"You liar, you fucking piece of shit!" Scorpion screamed over and over again as he was being hauled away by three corrections officers, with his wrists cuffed behind his back. He struggled against their stronghold, twisting, turning, and kicking his legs wildly. He was acting a goddamn fool inside of that visitors' room and didn't show any signs of slowing down.

The corrections officers assisted Othman back upon his feet. He stood between them, rubbing his neck and looking at Scorpion being drug away.

"Paperchase would never do that to me, you lying bastard!" Scorpion screamed again. "You fucked with the wrong one. Now you'll pay! You're a dead man! You hear me? You're a dead man!"

To Be Continued
King of the Trenches 2
Coming Soon

Submission Guideline

Submit the first three chapters of your completed manuscript to
ldpsubmissions@gmail.com, subject line: Your book's title. The
manuscript must be in a .doc file and sent as an attachment. Document
should be in Times New Roman, double spaced and in size 12 font. Also,
provide your synopsis and full contact information. If sending multiple
submissions, they must each be in a separate email.

Have a story but no way to send it electronically? You can still submit to
LDP/Ca$h Presents. Send in the first three chapters, written or typed, of
your completed manuscript to:

LDP: Submissions Dept
Po Box 944
Stockbridge, Ga 30281

DO NOT send original manuscript. Must be a duplicate.

Provide your synopsis and a cover letter containing your full contact
information.

Thanks for considering LDP and Ca$h Presents.

NEW RELEASES

MOB TIES 3 by SAYNOMORE
CONFESSIONS OF A GANGSTA by NICHOLAS LOCK
MURDA WAS THE CASE by ELIJAH R. FREEMAN
THE STREETS NEVER LET GO by ROBERT BAPTISTE
MOBBED UP 4 by KING RIO
AN UNFORESEEN LOVE 2 by MEESHA
KING OF THE TRENCHES by GHOST & TRANAY ADAMS

Ghost & Tranay Adams

<u>Coming Soon from Lock Down Publications/Ca$h Presents</u>
BLOOD OF A BOSS **VI**
SHADOWS OF THE GAME II
TRAP BASTARD II
By **Askari**
LOYAL TO THE GAME **IV**
By **T.J. & Jelissa**
IF TRUE SAVAGE **VIII**
MIDNIGHT CARTEL IV
DOPE BOY MAGIC IV
CITY OF KINGZ III
NIGHTMARE ON SILENT AVE II
By **Chris Green**
BLAST FOR ME **III**
A SAVAGE DOPEBOY III
CUTTHROAT MAFIA III
DUFFLE BAG CARTEL VII
HEARTLESS GOON VI
By **Ghost**
A HUSTLER'S DECEIT III
KILL ZONE II
BAE BELONGS TO ME III
By **Aryanna**
COKE KINGS V
KING OF THE TRAP III
By **T.J. Edwards**
GORILLAZ IN THE BAY V
3X KRAZY III
De'Kari
KINGPIN KILLAZ IV

King of the Trenches

STREET KINGS III

PAID IN BLOOD III

CARTEL KILLAZ IV

DOPE GODS III

Hood Rich

SINS OF A HUSTLA II

ASAD

RICH $AVAGE II

By Troublesome

YAYO V

Bred In The Game 2

S. Allen

CREAM III

By Yolanda Moore

SON OF A DOPE FIEND III

HEAVEN GOT A GHETTO II

By Renta

LOYALTY AIN'T PROMISED III

By Keith Williams

I'M NOTHING WITHOUT HIS LOVE II

SINS OF A THUG II

TO THE THUG I LOVED BEFORE II

By Monet Dragun

QUIET MONEY IV

EXTENDED CLIP III

THUG LIFE IV

By **Trai'Quan**

THE STREETS MADE ME IV

By **Larry D. Wright**

IF YOU CROSS ME ONCE II

By **Anthony Fields**
THE STREETS WILL NEVER CLOSE II
By **K'ajji**
HARD AND RUTHLESS III
THE BILLIONAIRE BENTLEYS II
Von Diesel
KILLA KOUNTY II
By **Khufu**
MONEY GAME II
By **Smoove Dolla**
A GANGSTA'S KARMA II
By **FLAME**
JACK BOYZ VERSUS DOPE BOYZ
By **Romell Tukes**
MOB TIES IV
By **SayNoMore**
MURDA WAS THE CASE II
Elijah R. Freeman
THE STREETS NEVER LET GO II
By **Robert Baptiste**
AN UNFORESEEN LOVE III
By **Meesha**
KING OF THE TRENCHES II
by **GHOST & TRANAY ADAMS**

Available Now

RESTRAINING ORDER **I & II**
By **CA$H & Coffee**
LOVE KNOWS NO BOUNDARIES **I II & III**
By **Coffee**
RAISED AS A GOON I, II, III & IV
BRED BY THE SLUMS I, II, III
BLAST FOR ME I & II
ROTTEN TO THE CORE I II III
A BRONX TALE I, II, III
DUFFLE BAG CARTEL I II III IV V VI
HEARTLESS GOON I II III IV V
A SAVAGE DOPEBOY I II
DRUG LORDS I II III
CUTTHROAT MAFIA I II
KING OF THE TRENCHES
By **Ghost**
LAY IT DOWN **I & II**
LAST OF A DYING BREED I II
BLOOD STAINS OF A SHOTTA I & II III
By **Jamaica**
LOYAL TO THE GAME I II III
LIFE OF SIN I, II III
By **TJ & Jelissa**
BLOODY COMMAS I & II
SKI MASK CARTEL I II & III
KING OF NEW YORK I II,III IV V
RISE TO POWER I II III
COKE KINGS I II III IV
BORN HEARTLESS I II III IV

KING OF THE TRAP I II

By **T.J. Edwards**

IF LOVING HIM IS WRONG…I & II

LOVE ME EVEN WHEN IT HURTS I II III

By **Jelissa**

WHEN THE STREETS CLAP BACK I & II III

THE HEART OF A SAVAGE I II III

By **Jibril Williams**

A DISTINGUISHED THUG STOLE MY HEART I II & III

LOVE SHOULDN'T HURT I II III IV

RENEGADE BOYS I II III IV

PAID IN KARMA I II III

SAVAGE STORMS I II

AN UNFORESEEN LOVE I II

By **Meesha**

A GANGSTER'S CODE I &, II III

A GANGSTER'S SYN I II III

THE SAVAGE LIFE I II III

CHAINED TO THE STREETS I II III

BLOOD ON THE MONEY I II III

By J-Blunt

PUSH IT TO THE LIMIT

By **Bre' Hayes**

BLOOD OF A BOSS **I, II, III, IV, V**

SHADOWS OF THE GAME

TRAP BASTARD

By **Askari**

THE STREETS BLEED MURDER **I, II & III**

THE HEART OF A GANGSTA I II& III

By **Jerry Jackson**

King of the Trenches

CUM FOR ME I II III IV V VI VII
An **LDP Erotica Collaboration**
BRIDE OF A HUSTLA **I II & II**
THE FETTI GIRLS **I, II& III**
CORRUPTED BY A GANGSTA I, II III, IV
BLINDED BY HIS LOVE
THE PRICE YOU PAY FOR LOVE I, II ,III
DOPE GIRL MAGIC I II III
By **Destiny Skai**
WHEN A GOOD GIRL GOES BAD
By **Adrienne**
THE COST OF LOYALTY I II III
By Kweli
A GANGSTER'S REVENGE **I II III & IV**
THE BOSS MAN'S DAUGHTERS I II III IV V
A SAVAGE LOVE **I & II**
DAE BELONGS TO ME I II
A HUSTLER'S DECEIT I, II, III
WHAT BAD BITCHES DO I, II, III
SOUL OF A MONSTER I II III
KILL ZONE
A DOPE BOY'S QUEEN I II III
By **Aryanna**
A KINGPIN'S AMBITON
A KINGPIN'S AMBITION **II**
I MURDER FOR THE DOUGH
By **Ambitious**
TRUE SAVAGE I II III IV V VI VII
DOPE BOY MAGIC I, II, III
MIDNIGHT CARTEL I II III

CITY OF KINGZ I II

NIGHTMARE ON SILENT AVE

By **Chris Green**

A DOPEBOY'S PRAYER

By **Eddie "Wolf" Lee**

THE KING CARTEL **I, II & III**

By **Frank Gresham**

THESE NIGGAS AIN'T LOYAL **I, II & III**

By **Nikki Tee**

GANGSTA SHYT **I II &III**

By **CATO**

THE ULTIMATE BETRAYAL

By **Phoenix**

BOSS'N UP **I , II & III**

By **Royal Nicole**

I LOVE YOU TO DEATH

By **Destiny J**

I RIDE FOR MY HITTA

I STILL RIDE FOR MY HITTA

By **Misty Holt**

LOVE & CHASIN' PAPER

By **Qay Crockett**

TO DIE IN VAIN

SINS OF A HUSTLA

By **ASAD**

BROOKLYN HUSTLAZ

By **Boogsy Morina**

BROOKLYN ON LOCK I & II

By **Sonovia**

GANGSTA CITY

King of the Trenches

By **Teddy Duke**
A DRUG KING AND HIS DIAMOND I & II III
A DOPEMAN'S RICHES
HER MAN, MINE'S TOO I, II
CASH MONEY HO'S
THE WIFEY I USED TO BE I II
By Nicole Goosby
TRAPHOUSE KING **I II & III**
KINGPIN KILLAZ I II III
STREET KINGS I II
PAID IN BLOOD **I II**
CARTEL KILLAZ I II III
DOPE GODS I II
By **Hood Rich**
LIPSTICK KILLAH **I, II, III**
CRIME OF PASSION I II & III
FRIEND OR FOE I II III
By **Mimi**
STEADY MOBBN' **I, II, III**
THE STREETS STAINED MY SOUL I II
By **Marcellus Allen**
WHO SHOT YA **I, II, III**
SON OF A DOPE FIEND I II
HEAVEN GOT A GHETTO
Renta
GORILLAZ IN THE BAY **I II III IV**
TEARS OF A GANGSTA I II
3X KRAZY I II
DE'KARI
TRIGGADALE I II III

MURDAROBER WAS THE CASE
Elijah R. Freeman
GOD BLESS THE TRAPPERS I, II, III
THESE SCANDALOUS STREETS I, II, III
FEAR MY GANGSTA I, II, III IV, V
THESE STREETS DON'T LOVE NOBODY I, II
BURY ME A G I, II, III, IV, V
A GANGSTA'S EMPIRE I, II, III, IV
THE DOPEMAN'S BODYGAURD I II
THE REALEST KILLAZ I II III
THE LAST OF THE OGS I II III
Tranay Adams
THE STREETS ARE CALLING
Duquie Wilson
MARRIED TO A BOSS I II III
By Destiny Skai & Chris Green
KINGZ OF THE GAME I II III IV V
Playa Ray
SLAUGHTER GANG I II III
RUTHLESS HEART I II III
By Willie Slaughter
FUK SHYT
By Blakk Diamond
DON'T F#CK WITH MY HEART I II
By Linnea
ADDICTED TO THE DRAMA I II III
IN THE ARM OF HIS BOSS II
By Jamila
YAYO I II III IV
A SHOOTER'S AMBITION I II

King of the Trenches

BRED IN THE GAME
By S. Allen
TRAP GOD I II III
RICH $AVAGE
By Troublesome
FOREVER GANGSTA
GLOCKS ON SATIN SHEETS I II
By Adrian Dulan
TOE TAGZ I II III
LEVELS TO THIS SHYT I II
By Ah'Million
KINGPIN DREAMS I II III
By Paper Boi Rari
CONFESSIONS OF A GANGSTA I II III IV
By Nicholas Lock
I'M NOTHING WITHOUT HIS LOVE
SINS OF A THUG
TO THE THUG I LOVED BEFORE
By Monet Dragun
CAUGHT UP IN THE LIFE I II III
THE STREETS NEVER LET GO
By Robert Baptiste
NEW TO THE GAME I II III
MONEY, MURDER & MEMORIES I II III
By **Malik D. Rice**
LIFE OF A SAVAGE I II III
A GANGSTA'S QUR'AN I II III
MURDA SEASON I II III
GANGLAND CARTEL I II III
CHI'RAQ GANGSTAS I II III

KILLERS ON ELM STREET I II III

JACK BOYZ N DA BRONX I II III

A DOPEBOY'S DREAM

By **Romell Tukes**

LOYALTY AIN'T PROMISED I II

By Keith Williams

QUIET MONEY I II III

THUG LIFE I II III

EXTENDED CLIP I II

By **Trai'Quan**

THE STREETS MADE ME I II III

By **Larry D. Wright**

THE ULTIMATE SACRIFICE I, II, III, IV, V, VI

KHADIFI

IF YOU CROSS ME ONCE

ANGEL I II

IN THE BLINK OF AN EYE

By **Anthony Fields**

THE LIFE OF A HOOD STAR

By Ca$h & Rashia Wilson

THE STREETS WILL NEVER CLOSE

By K'ajji

CREAM I II

By Yolanda Moore

NIGHTMARES OF A HUSTLA I II III

By King Dream

CONCRETE KILLA I II

By Kingpen

HARD AND RUTHLESS I II

MOB TOWN 251

King of the Trenches

THE BILLIONAIRE BENTLEYS
By Von Diesel
GHOST MOB
Stilloan Robinson
MOB TIES I II III
By SayNoMore
BODYMORE MURDERLAND I II III
By Delmont Player
FOR THE LOVE OF A BOSS
By C. D. Blue
MOBBED UP I II III IV
By King Rio
KILLA KOUNTY
By Khufu
MONEY GAME
By Smoove Dolla
A GANGSTA'S KARMA
By FLAME
KING OF THE TRENCHES II
by **GHOST & TRANAY ADAMS**

BOOKS BY LDP'S CEO, CA$H

TRUST IN NO MAN

TRUST IN NO MAN 2

TRUST IN NO MAN 3

BONDED BY BLOOD

SHORTY GOT A THUG

THUGS CRY

THUGS CRY 2

THUGS CRY 3

TRUST NO BITCH

TRUST NO BITCH 2

TRUST NO BITCH 3

TIL MY CASKET DROPS

RESTRAINING ORDER

RESTRAINING ORDER 2

IN LOVE WITH A CONVICT

LIFE OF A HOOD STAR

King of the Trenches